The Other Side of Stone

LINDA CRACKNELL

TAPROOT PRESS

First published by Taproot Press 2021

ISBN: 978-1-8380800-1-3

Printed and bound by Bell & Bain Ltd., Glasgow.

Typeset in 11 point Garamond by Main Point Books, Edinburgh

Cover design by Ignacio Paul https://nachoandrespaul.myportfolio.com

Contents

For Robin,
and in memory of my mother 1931–2020

1831

Stone Curse

Some days it's just the wee fellow who watches me. I see him through the hazel-arch of the workshop when I turn my head, and he's there when I take my tools out to the forge to be licked sharp in the flames. He perches on the top of the rubble pile, or on a post, and observes. A smart-looker he is, with his white collar and chestnut stomach. Out of his dark face comes a scolding cry when there's someone coming. He's an unquiet bird then, with his 'clack-clack-clack,' for all as if he's bashing two stones together.

If the women hear him they turn their backs, pull their caps over their cheeks like blinkers, wondering who the *rosad* will fall upon.

'Will it be your father who wakes up blind?' I tease them as they go by. 'Or your man that falls from a crag and loses the use of his legs? Or maybe the leg in-between will drop off!'

It's not for a man of my age to be feared of a bird the size of my thumb. And the fellow's my friend is he not? He's my steady companion, watching me force the chisel upon this rock that's so brute-hard my scours and drafts will be there to see for centuries to come.

Other days it seems I've the whole village gathered about me – the Camerons and MacGregors and Macfarlanes. There's this rare excitement lighting up the place, the blether and rumours dashing between cottages. Folk flock about here, any time of day or night, quite bespelled by the thing clambering towards the heavens in steel and wood and stone.

They whisper about the man on the horse, come from the south to build a new mountain in their midst, bringing wool-spinners under the one pitched roof to make them all rich. Of course we've heard of whole forests of machinery-mills going up in the south, but to have such a thing here all on its own has them quite puffed up. The glamour of it's rosied their cheeks and has them bobbing and smiling when the man comes by to see progress. An awe-struck hush comes upon them save for those who've a few words of the English.

He has a quiet way about him, and a good smile, and they say he speaks of new markets and the 'fancy' trade for trousers, and protective checks for the estates. The Minister tells me the man wishes to stop a trade as well as to start one. He has important business as far away as London, where he must join with other grand men to bring freedom to African people sold as slaves.

As they've got used to me, the men have started to bring their whisky and stories into the workshop. At first they stayed on their feet, but these days they each squat on a piece of rubble they've brought in from the pile. And I keep on with my work on the dressings, easing my stiff legs as I stretch to reach the whole length of the slab, taming it into smooth lines. It's to be the dedication stone above the door that holds the whole thing up.

On the inside of my head I speak with the stone, listen to

its testimony, while the men's stories chip away on the outside. I keep at it till the gloaming or the whisky steal the features from its face. Or when the rattles and gurgles in my lungs pull me down, and I wrench the cloth from my mouth, and join the men.

As I shake the white-finger from my hand, they put their questions upon me about where I've come from, and how it was to work on the grand tower all those years at Taymouth, the castle they still call 'Slippery John's'. Pinned in an ice-scoured valley it was, I say, with a rocky ridge on each side. We were building up through four floors to try and get out of the shade in winter. But the topping-out, well that was a fair day, so it was.

Then they ask me about my road here. 'Which one did you take, journeyman?' they want to know. And I know why they ask. I've heard of folk who'll go the long way round to avoid the ford at Loch an Daim and the fear of having the flesh torn from them. Even myself, I took care to get over it before nightfall, with my slow shuffle from the far valley jarred and halted all the way by the cough. Surely it'll be my last journey to find work, surely my last.

They tell me about this weaver they knew, coming that way, over the shoulder of the hill in daylight, and how he called at a nearby cottage for directions. He met a man there, tall and lean, a schoolmaster so he said, all alone. The weaver was persuaded to stay a while for a drink and so was belated.

As the weaver crossed the ford between loch and cliff just after the gloaming, he heard hooves coming towards him on the polished track, cloven hooves, and found himself faced by a goat on its hind legs with cat's claws for hands, dog's fangs and a human face. But this weaver had a special weapon. To the schoolmaster he'd called it his 'cat behind the hip' – the *sgian dubh* was what he meant – and this goat-demon wasn't expecting the blade he took in his chest, went roaring off into the night with a great frothing and gurgling of blood in his throat.

The travelling weaver ran back to the schoolmaster's cottage for help, and what did he find? Nothing but the schoolmaster lying in bed and his life leaving him from a wound in his chest. The weaver hurried on down here to the village and gave the bell-man something to shout the next morning.

'The cat behind the hip': it's a fine way of calling it.

'We should put that story on young Archie there,' one of the old boys cackles, for not one of them can recall now, exactly who this weaver was. The story needs a new subject. He points over at the lad with the raven hair and shock-blue eyes. We're all sitting in gloom, warmed with the lantern and mixing whisky-mist breath, and I see the lad's hands twisting a dance with each other but also his wee grim smile. He comes in with the men these days, since his da's away with the fever.

'He's needing a turn as the hero, is he not?' The old boy cackles on. 'Then the lassies'll flock to him like the starlings at even.'

I leave my own work at intervals during the day, when my back's stabbed with needles from leaning too long over the banker. I take a stroll around the other masons at their work. They've stones just a small size compared to mine, coloured dark or sand or even pale blue. They're levelling them so they'll sit one over the other right up into the sky. You have to understand the pull of the earth to get that right. Masons are like God in that way I always think. I take a look at each, weigh it with my ancient eye, give the man my nod or a word.

But there's one I stare at while he works. When he steps back,

I cough up a great gobbet of spittle and aim it at the top face of his rock. The wet brings out those tiny flecks of red that sometimes worm in this strange, hard stone.

Mason to mason, this young man steels his accusing eyes into mine, still a midgie on a mountain in his understanding. His lips are pushed into a purse of indignation. The gobbet slicks towards the ground making a long, stained line of charcoal. He's still to learn respect, to know that each day for the rock is measured in a man's million years.

'That bed's not straight,' I say, pointing at the top side, and walk away with the chick's eyes burrowing into my back, as he digests his lesson.

I go back to my own slab, its long straight grey back made perfectly flat, the beds and joints already prepared to fit the place of pride above the door. I'm ready to start the face now, and the four bearded fixers come, levering it over to expose the last untreated surface. I take up the boaster.

Later, the wee fellow clacks his warning outside, and there's young Archie, putting his blue eyes on me, and his hand on the rock. It's a soft hand yet, without my knobbled joints and skin cracked to weeping with the cold and heat and the rough care of the stone. He wants to learn, he says, and so he starts to come each day to watch between his chores, just like the wee fellow perched outside.

He gets used to speaking, when his elders aren't about, and he tells me of a lass on their farm, her dress the colour of new birch leaves, and her hair bright yellow like the whins aflame. Tall and thin, he says, and she watches the cows without being asked to. His mother pours milk into the hollow of a rock at the gateway each evening, and by the morning it's supped quite clean away.

'And you've seen her,' I say. 'Have you spoken?'

But he's only glanced her from the corner of his eye, he says, as she goes between the cattle and the loch. I nod, and recognise in myself the first fret gnawing.

He comes out with me to the forge and I show him how to heat the chisels till they're rowanberry-red, then douse the steel in water for its angry display of spit and steam, to see the colour of the temper. 'See,' I say. 'When it's cooled – as blue as a raven's wing – it's fit for anything.'

He says he'll remember that.

'And you've to be careful with the lassies, you'll remember that well too?' I warn him.

Next time the man on the horse comes, his son rides next to him, barely older than Archie I suppose, but acting like a man of business. I shake my head at the father, in place of words of the English, at the picture he brings of his family monogram for the dedication stone. I sweep my fingers around its curves and intricacies. It'll be a carver he wants, not a master-mason, to give him that. I show him by tapping a point with the mallet, how easily it slips off the cruel hardness of this local stone. I could manage to carve the pen of course, but what we do not share the words for, I cannot say to him – why would anyone wish a crow to decorate their building? He hangs his head, stops his smiling for a minute, nodding bitterly at his son.

But the next day back they come with a new idea, a simpler one. The year. That's all that's needed for a dedication stone. The smile flicks across his face like sun on the hill on a wild March day, and the son laughs and laughs when he sees that I agree. The father even draws it for me on a piece of wood, as if I can't carry the shape in my own head. I like to keep designs in there so the carving appears as a miracle of sorts, folk gathering to see, ducking the shards flying from the chisel in case they should seek out cheek or eye. But that's when I'm working with slate, the luxury of butter, not this cruel stone.

'Better you'd built it in 1741 or 1477,' I find a way to say by showing him the ease of making straight lines on a length of timber. But 1831 has been chosen with all its double curves, and this stone has been chosen, hacked from the earth and dragged here by oxen as quarry block. A fine stone since they're thinking to plant something permanent and wise here. I see how the land's been captured from marsh, the water sucked from it and gathered with that fall of the river to make a fast channel to drive the wheel.

Each day villagers' necks crane back further to see the top as the stone gathers upwards to dwarf the church and build a spectacle. The shadow we cast grows daily, stretching out across the grass and the felled apple orchard towards the Inn and the row of cottages. It's got the mouth of the Campbell woman flickering up and down like the wee bird's tail, as she stands in her doorway knee-deep in children, half agleed, half afeared, now the sun has been blocked from her cottage.

Young Archie comes back, hand on the stone and an eye on me, like he's trying to draw wisdom from us both. He's telling me how his mother's become firm, saying now her man is cold she's not able to spare milk for a good-for-nothing lass. The rock under my hand tells me he will speak of missing calves or dead babies. But he just says how he misses seeing the lass.

'Would you not be better to give your eye to the young MacGregor girl with her long hair, or the one who has a strawberry for a mouth, and hair to match?' I say. For the other, I think, will rove, choosing to cause harm or not as the fancy takes her.

I nod away his hand, pull the cloth back over my mouth, and give the chisel to the stone.

The younger horse-man comes back again and takes us by surprise in the workshop, so that The Smuggler has to hurry out with a keg bulged under his coat and his cheeks still swollen with a gobful. The father is in London stopping one business whilst the building of another is entrusted to his son. I show him with my hand how I've smoothed the face with the boaster, and how it's ready now for carving. We both stare at it. It's a rock that has different things to reveal – its glint or its darkness under certain lights or drenches. He comes close and lays his face against it. It's like he's kissing it or whispering a secret.

It puts me in mind of that story the men tell of the reiver come from the north who on his way falls for a lassie minding a favourite cow. When she asked for the third time where he came from and what his business was, he could not hold out, and so instead of telling her, he unburdened himself by whispering it to the cow. 'Black cow, come midnight, you'll be half the way to Lochaber,' he said. He wasn't to know the lassie was the Laird's daughter, her ears sharp, and so the cottage-folk were armed and ready for the raid. It was a black night alright for Lochaber.

Whisper to a cow if you will, but whispering to a rock will do less than a dog-rose petal touching the crag up there as it floats downwards, swinging this way and then that like a wee boat caught in the wind. Isn't the hardest strike I can make with my bolster as weak to this rock as a single kiss? But then the young fellow feels in his pocket and brings out a swatch of woollen fabric, puts it against the stone, and sure enough if you squint your eye, it's of a colour with it, in tiny checks of grey, black and brown. We catch eyes and out of him tumbles his laugh that sparks up my own.

Archie comes back speaking of a calf pushed away by its mother. They gave it the amulet but there's some stronger magic at work, for she still rejected it. So the calf has folded its legs under itself, and is weak-lidded about the eyes. A frown has drawn itself across Archie's brow as he watches me turn the curves of the '3' with the point.

When I look aside to Archie's eyes, I see the whins still blazing in their reflection. She still plays her mischief.

The next day he comes, and the calf has died. The family are saddened without new life about them and have lost the promise of a sale. He looks to the building and asks when it will be finished, when will there be work?

Worse news comes. There's a wee brother, Robbie, who sometimes trails after Archie, a match for him in raven and blue. He likes to play on the floor, building and balancing stones or chippings, one above the other, or enjoying the weight of my tools and laying them out in a long line. Robbie is now roaring with a fever. Archie's face takes on the frowns and wrinkles of ancient rock.

'Would your mother not think of putting out the milk again?' I ask him.

But the cow has dried up.

He goes away round-shouldered and slow while my lungs rattle and erupt, stealing speech.

I look at the patient rock that waits with its face up, the year I've marked upon it like a flea-bite in its story. I dust off the surface, and see that it is fine, that the light will catch it almost as from a plate of silver. And on the top bed, where it will be hidden, I make my mark; a straight line topped with a pointing triangle, and two more hanging from one side. It will breathe secretly in the joint against the stone above.

Then I think of the lad, so young to be so troubled, and the lass, the *glaistig*, displaced and vengeful. It brings a cold cloak-mist about my shoulders.

The four beards come at my summons and roll the stone over, lifting with bent, trembling legs. The back of the stone now faces upwards on the banker. I nod them away to be alone with it. My guard, the wee fellow with the white collar chapping on his pile of rubble, is the only one who sees what I do. The plan of it is already carved in my mind. The long lines of an A-shaped dress on a figure tall and thin. Her face straight-edged, hair a series of small chips spiking from her head like a halo of flames. A chip kissed into the stone for each eye, and for a mouth.

Then the beards are carrying the stone to its place, sliding it up the prepared planks, too hard-muscled and lung-blown to notice my extra design. She is turned to face inwards, hidden against iron and timber whilst the proud date-inscribed face meets the world, like a bell-man proclaiming a revolution. A scattered cheer goes up and a keg is passed low between the men who've paused in their work.

I begin to gather my tools into the bag, checking they are all there by number and all carry my mark. When I leave the workshop I sense an absence. There's no sign of my smart-looking friend, the bird. Perhaps he will clack his stones and make his new guard atop the growing grey walls.

I look west towards the loch which will power this place, and towards the lad's farm. I suck on a hope that his family will be free of the *glaistig* now that I've given her a place to stay. And then a cough takes me and bends me double, and it's a few moments before I can straighten up again, ready to be on my way.

January 1913

In and Out the Windows

Come on, give me a keek of that husband of mine. What have you done with him, then? I don't see him framed in his usual window, bent over the loom. I've to show him this, see, come in this morning's post. It's got a crest that my finger bumps over. A crest, aye. And it's addressed to me. To me.

Maybe you don't hear me, with all that great rattling and jumping going on inside you, and the engine outside puffing and panting to keep up with the machines. Never as keen for a blether as me, eh?

You've a face like a keekin gless the day, all your watery eyes catching at the falling sun. Does it not make you feel a wee bit in danger, all that glass? But you've your bell-towers to make you feel important. One for east and one for west, bringing the whole village to squeeze like a swarm of bees into that door and up your stairwell. Oh aye, you're the rare wee tyrant.

And I'm here waiting again. On my bench. But I'm early today, right enough.

I know them by heart now, your windows. Nine across the top floor, then nine from right to left on your next, and so on to the bottom corner, four floors down. Counting's a fine way to pass the time – to take my mind off the cold chewing my fingertips.

In and out the windows
In and out the windows
In and out the windows
One, two, three.

I know your lines and wrinkles too, by sight if not by touch. Those patches of oil staining your stone to black. The wee curve made in the stonework at the top of each window. It's just how I've got to know the laugh lines of John's face. It's from staring into it each night by the fire, when we measure our fingers against each other's. Under his nails there's aye the wool-grease to scrape out, and under mine the bannock-dough, terrible stuff that sets solid like stone. It goes with this rattle. You hear? Aye, a box of matches in my apron pocket to show the proper wee country wife I'm becoming. We laugh about that in between talking about meetings I've been at and women getting pelted with eggs and men's crude words for their trouble, all as if they were hoors, not suffragettes.

Aye, then, play me your tune while I wait. Now, is it a jig or reel? We've the looms two-stepping on the first two floors, and then the whirr of the twisting frames above. But the spinning mule, there on the top floor, that's harmony, eh? Making its wee dance with the operative as they glide in and out.

And there's the river all solemn and slow behind you, not seeming to mind what you steal from it for your lade, and the splashing wheel that turns and turns at the same speed all day, till I find myself inside it, my eyes dropping shut with the turn and splash, turn and splash.

What a joke, eh? That we chose you instead of a ship to

Canada? Glunchy old you, sat still and sour-faced. I could just picture myself, when I read the adverts, on a sleek, shiny, new ship. I'd be the one stood at the prow, cutting through the waves, the first to spy the land of opportunities.

We went down to the Clyde even, saw one of them away. Folk were cheek-by-jowl on the decks, greetin and waving, and the noise was rising off them across the water. And the hankies all like wee blossoms shaken about in the March wind.

It's you that's our ship now. A big square grey stone ship. So where is it we're sailing to?

I mind the windows back in Neilston too. Alexander's Mill, sunk down below the line of the hill with its zig-zags of climbing stairs clinging to the outside walls, and all its different faces, and windows different shapes and sizes. It was as jaggy as the Paisley skyline itself with all its towers and chimneys.

And we spinners running along, singing and shouting up at the windows. A river, so we were, with our bunnets catching the sun to make a field of flowers. Aye and the polis trying to push us back. Five thousand we were, according to the papers. And all because five girls were doing the work of six. And that damn feartie Maister Hough hiding in the railway station for his precious life.

Hearken to this part. A wee lesson for you. There was a woman, stopped the flow. Aye, and she had a great rock in her hand, heavy and rough. It wheeshed high over the heads of the lassies and the polis helmets, clattering through a first-floor window. Then she caught my eye, said she should follow it in with a burning clootie, eh? And then there was shattering and shrieks, and ducking heads as we all followed her example. Aye, but later we got the assurances we wanted from the bosses. It worked, see. And all they could do was put wire mesh over the windows.

You're no as big and bold as a cotton mill in Paisley, but still, for a wee village stuck here in the back of nowhere, you're something. And right enough you dwarf the white cottages on either side of you. Even the hotel and the hall down the road, the kirk, almost everything in the place. You squeeze them quite breathless.

But don't you go thinking that coming here was my first choice. It was John's mother, aye, and the sisters, wanted him back here at the weaving, after his da and his grandpa. Stone dead they are in the graveyard down the road but John couldn't resist coming to see, when he got the offer from your Maister Knight. And that was the once I was allowed inside. For the guided tour. Once! With all the la-di-da politeness and old Maister Knight pointing at the stone above your door to show us how long ago you were made.

No-one warned me about the smell of you mind, like a clootie in my face, smothering my words. You could sink your fingernails into a smell like that – greasy and thick, like the sheen you send home on John's clothes, and on those rows of tweed samples in his precious pattern book. He says he doesn't smell it anymore, but I do. I've noticed as well how his forelock's grown, so it limps over his eyes.

Aye, don't think I've not noticed what you're up to.

After our wee trip to the country, he came on that persuasive, said we can live in new ways, Catharine, amongst the old ones. And we can carry the new ideas out to the provinces. We don't need to go to Canada for a new start. And I wasn't so sure.

But that's when I telt him of that other idea, seeing as how we both believe in a woman's right to work, married or no. The idea that's smouldering here under my shawl. And he said aye, why not, we can talk about it once we're there.

Is it that your Maister-Knight-Sir's caught him into the office? He must come out soon, eh? I've his favourite tea waiting at home. We'll walk back together arm in arm, you watch. I'll wind a skein of your finest wool around his shoulders, reel him to me until his eye's matching my eye, his smile to my smile, and I'll show him what's been burning my hand all day. A wee keek at it and I'll be on the road to a proper training. I'll be making myself into a nurse, and I'll be the one to say what happens to my person and my time and my money.

All I need is his signature.

It's dark so early in this winter village. All your rows of lit windows are glowing brighter, the lassies on show up on the third floor, their heads bent like they're praying to the twisting frames. No idea, those lassies, eh? No notion of that fairy hill, with its daft wee point way above their heads – the rust, purple, and the steel-grey rock all fading into the gloaming. Not one of them's taught themselves to read and write, I bet. Maybe they've not heard yet about the labour movement, or even about suffrage.

They'll still be jangling, no doubt, from the swarry on Saturday night, all the flushed faces from the dancing and the whisky, the pretty gowns ballooning out. We were reeling till two in the morning. There'll be new clicks to giggle about I'll bet. And you'll be leaning in your great fat walls, sooking up their whispers between the twisting frames.

The 'happy family' Maister Knight cried us from his platform.

The happy family. Jings!

'Hand in hand, the proper relation between employer and employee,' he said, 'so we can prosper together.'

Hold my John's hand, I thought, and you'll get yourself a slap.

And then one of the foremen was up on his hind legs, thanking them for inviting us all and for their kindness through the last year. Aye, the kindness of oppressors and capitalists. So out of me comes a snort, like I was that Krakatoa.

It was quite the dig in the ribs John gave me. And just after that he was piping up himself, and I thought the good socialist, he's going to speak up just like he did at those Glasgow meetings when I fell for him. And what does he do? He proposes a toast.

'Long life, happiness, and an increasing gathering every year,' he calls out.

My words clashed and clattered in my head, but none came out. Then he sat back down and whispered to me the news, that he'd been made a foreman.

My mouth hanging open, I'm pushed into the parade for the Gay Gordons. We step the backward bit inside our cradle of arms, and then I'm spinning, spinning, spinning, all dizzy and catching for my breath under his raised arm. We stride off thigh to thigh for all like our days marching under the banner in Glasgow. We're reeled together into the polka and match each other, step for step. The rough edges of him catch on my wrist and chin, and there's a wee spark in his eye that promises we'll be awake a while back home.

I mind my hands on his cotton shirt after the dance. I get one of they wee hot skitters to think on it. His breathing coming faster in my ear.

'You're not turning soft, are you, agreeing to be foreman and all?' I noticed the waxy look of his face then. 'You're not bowing to the bosses?'

But he whispers something about it being different here in the country, a family affair, and how there's growth in the market what with the demand for khaki and that. Coorie in, and I'll whisper you what happens next. Your lanolin keeps his hands soft as a wean's. I've no complaints there. So maybe I should thank you, eh?

You're not shocked – blushing up pink in the sunset? It's a secret between us, because we share the man, me and you. But you can't say you need him more than me just now, you mean old scallywag.

You'll not reply? You don't hear?

You'll tell me next you never heard those men earlier. That'll be why you did nothing to stand up for me, eh? Those beasts. Swaying and surly from the public house.

'Suffragette. Suffering yet?' calls out one of them.

I can be strong. Breathe, breathe, chin up. Like Miss Parker with her grace under fire, aye.

'You nothing to do at home? Go and mind the bairns,' he says.

Snap. Snap goes the anger, and my tongue free as a snake.

'Aye. I could be a mother. Or a nurse, or a mill lassie, and yet not have the vote. Whereas you're a useless drunkard, and you still have it.' My face afire.

'If you were my wife, I'd give you poison,' the drunk one comes at me again, leering round.

'If I were your wife, I'd take it!' Spitting. Tongue rattling.

He lunges, but the other one cleeks his arm, and they roll away.

This village. Look at me, stuck with just you to talk to. Aye, even the mill lassies look away when they pass me, and I heard John's mother tell him he should catch my dress in the mangle, to stop me gadding off to meetings. And there's his sisters asking when I'll be with child. It seems John hasn't told them what we agreed, how bringing weans into the world means women lose their lives to domestic labours.

I have to shut my mouth before that rhyme escapes.

Holy mother we believe
without sin thou didst conceive:
Holy mother, so believing,
Let us sin without conceiving.

We're a united front, him and me. We are so. Don't give me that look. I'll hold him to it. When he came home the other night asking if it was pie or mince, and it wasn't there yet because I'd been away at a meeting, I felt his arms around me slacken a wee bit. I had to laugh. How can I change the world between cooking lunch and dinner, John Devlin? I said to him. And he kissed me and changed from talking pie to the betrayal of the Reform Bill.

It's me he has kisses for, not you, see? And kisses make me forget how I'm feart what it is you and Maister Knight are steeping him in. He's my John, eh? Mine, not yours. You hear? And you can stop lanking his hair with grease, and sagging him with that tiredness he brings home.

He minds me of the effigy of Maister Hough the men marched onto the football field behind Alexander's that night, his arms cleeked between them, feet dragging behind, head bent and bobbing. There was thousands of us gathered, and that wee one with a red face stood up on a platform spitting out, 'Is he guilty?', as he shook the jointless, flopping man with its suit and tie and hat and a blank for a face. Three times he shouted it out, and every time the roar came up from the crowd. 'Aye. Aye.' Louder and more hungry each time. And then the last. One great roar it was that joined us all together, we were so set for justice. 'Aye!'

And then the paraffin was splashed, and great flames licked up and the wee jointless man was hoist onto it, and you've never heard such monstrous cheering this side of hell, and the bonfire a great mountain pointing up into the sky that you could see right across Scotland, I'd say.

Aye it's a fine warning to the bosses. These days John looks up a bit sharp-like when I says that.

You'll make me into the shivering ghost waiting for him at the end of the world on this bench. You old bitch.

I've made a wee picture of you in my head. You think you'll go on forever don't you, just like the turn and turn of that water wheel, so long as the river runs? But no. I see you become a decrepit ruin, abandoned by everybody, your roof fallen in, and your walls tumbling down, your two bells fallen into the mud so they can't even peep. The land'll rise up and swallow you, take you back.

I see it, I see it.

There's crows too. Come to hang about on your roof, clanking their great feet on your head, singing you heeshie-baw. And I hear them because you're so still, your machines silent. And I can make myself one of the crows. It helps me wait. Flying in and out your windows. How many of the gaping black gashes can I soar through, where the glass used to be?

It wouldn't take much. A hurled rock could set off your downfall, or a wee spark out of my apron pocket, if you get too greedy – the night shifts there's been talk of, the 'efficiency'. I know what it is that word means.

I'm a spinner, mind, like the spider. You might think yourself a grand thing but I can snarl you up with cords spun as tough as steel.

Give me my husband back, sly witch.

What's that? You holding your breath?

Looms. Clattering to a halt, are they?

Twisting frames whining down. Aye.

Heads moving between the machines, heading for the stairs now. You spit them out into the half-light, the men swinging onto bicycles, the girls' heads bent in a blether. I tuck my ankles under the bench as they pass me. Here's my shawl pulled in against the shivers and, under it, the paper's crisp.

At last! My man's shape flickering between the looms. A shadow of his face under his arm at the window, looking out for me, the wee darling.

The gas-light fades in each of your eyes, and you begin to shiver yourself down for the night, just like you're a wee dragon curling up under that mountain. Ach, perhaps you're not so bad. I could almost sing you a lullaby.

And the hand-held lamp flickers his silhouette across windows; the greased forelock bobbing, unfamiliar. Down and down he comes, down the stairwell.

And then the door finally opens. And as it swings, it unleashes a great storm of beating wings in my throat, and so I stand up to give them more room. I'm ready for the new road ahead of me. Ready to walk home arm in arm. Ready to slide that pen into his hand.

1990

The Last Tweed

He'd been locked in for nearly two days when, once again, he paused in his work to slide the packet from the breast pocket of his overalls. It rattled slightly, telling George, as if he didn't know, that there was only one cigarette left. He lifted it to his nose and sniffed. Even through the box, the scent rekindled his ache, a scent as distinct as the smoky whiff of freshly woven tweed when he'd got his arms around a bale of it. The huff of oil and his fingers grazing coarse fibre would conjure up heather, lichen, granite, sheep, send him beyond these walls and windows to hug the Perthshire hills themselves.

He flicked open the lid so he could see the pale circle of the filtered end. The salivations started, just as they did when he sat on the sofa at home and the words 'King Prawn Korma' on the Indian takeaway menu prickled at the roof of his mouth and pulsed heat against his palate.

He took the cigarette out and rolled it between his fingers, raised it to his lips. It was slightly battered and bent from its previous parades. All that was wanting was the spark which would grant a deep sigh of relief.

But in here, with the oil-soaked timber, that spark was forbidden.

At first he'd restricted this *non*-smoking ritual to the times of the factory breaks. It was habit. The first at nine o'clock – traditional breakfast-time after an hour's work. The next was at eleven, then twelve-thirty for lunch and finally three o'clock in the afternoon, teatime.

When things were still normal, he would have put his break-time ciggie unlit into his mouth, paced down the steps, out of the heavy door, and up the path to the gate. The match striking out its tongue of sound and flame to turn paper, tobacco and himself into one breathing thing, wouldn't come until he was completely off the premises, on the street. He used to relish the expectation.

'George's King Size sway', that was what the other boys had called his short, stately walk. Or was it 'way' they'd been saying, he wondered now?

'Aye, right Regal,' he'd reply with an appropriate wave. He never hurried like them. He watched the lichen-like ash crumble and drift downwind until it was time to grind the butt under a heel.

He could stop the loom whenever he fancied now he was alone. The days of the clocking-in machine, and the siren screeching through all four floors when it was time to surge down the stairs were a distant memory, one the grandchildren might talk about at school. Just like they'd soon be able to talk about Ravenscraig – the great days of British Steel – and maybe with a bit of luck even the Iron Lady herself.

There was no-one around to look over his shoulder. The young poofter, Knight, had buggered off back to Edinburgh with the excuse of the bank or the insurers or the assessors.

Hadn't George heard the hammering of nails into coffins when the fluff-faced lad joined the firm three years earlier with a black hole for business sense after some arty-farty university degree? What good could he possibly be, despite his father's reassurances that the Mill was 'in his blood and in his bones'. At least his father had shifted with the times, known how to be a boss, not just shrugged his shoulders and accepted market collapse.

So it was he himself, George Kaye, who was now King Prawn. He seemed to be charged with laying all that had happened here properly to rest, showing a bit of respect to a business that had sustained the place for over a century and a half. But he'd got himself locked in with this thing squeezing its steel tentacles around his chest.

He went back to the loom and put on his ear defenders. The pattern book with its rows of estate tweed samples was lying open, each window an echo of the landscape – mottled greens, blues, gold and beige. Bracken, bluebells, primroses, and birch. He was working on a length for the Glen Alder Estate. An outstanding order. Proof that there was still life in the business. It had to be fifty yards long, and so far it was only twenty-five. This was the only mill in the country still delivering these short commissions. And still working on the old Dobcross looms at that.

He filled the pirn of pale blue yarn for a crossway that made up thirty-eight parts of the hundred, and replaced it in the shuttle. He thought of the oval recess inside as a womb, a strangely tender place within the grease-smoothed metal-tipped wooden bullet. He replaced the shuttle in its box, ready to cross and re-cross the warp that the shafts would open in sequence, determined by his careful threading the day before.

His stubby fingers worked at the loom, an echo of the first

jerks and twitches of his apprentice hands back in Huddersfield. But after thirty years, the movements were automatic and smooth, despite the increasingly crooked back and failing eyes. Today he took the greatest care, slowing and exaggerating each gesture as if he was demonstrating to an ignorant audience who knew bugger all about weaving. He slid the power bar across and the shuttles started their journey, slamming across from box to box in a ferocious display of speed and noise.

Visitors to the Mill always commented on it.

'How do you bear the noise?' they'd ask when he stopped it.

'Eh?' He'd crane his neck and cup his ear in their direction as they started to repeat it. 'I can't hear 'owt.'

There would never be any visitors now. He'd got used to the two floors hanging silently above him for the last ten years, and one yawning like a gloomy cellar below. But he knew fine well what would happen once the business was completely under wraps. The assessors wouldn't know one end of a loom from another, wouldn't know that they might be old enough to be valuable as museum artefacts – they'd end up as scrap.

Two days into his exile he was feeling quite at home. But when he went to fill the kettle at teatime, and nothing came out of the tap, his breath quickened. He knew enough about the IRA hunger strikes and the coal miners' tactics to be sure he would draw a line. He wasn't for those sort of heroics. You can't live without fluids. It forced him to make an inventory – a proper assessment of his situation. He still had a litre of Irn Bru left, and whatever water was sloshing about in the bottom of the kettle. Food-wise, he had half a packet of Jammy Dodgers, the remainder of his corned beef sandwiches, and a pork pie. How long would that give him?

The other boys had only been gone a week, he realised, and

might have left some scraps behind. On the windowsill next to Donny's loom he found a caramel wafer, still in its wrapper. Next to Andy's there was a Tupperware box, all closed up with a slightly inflated lid. Inside were two jam sandwiches, not mouldy yet. He tried not to think about the bite missing from one of them and Andy's yellowing teeth. It was only if he got really desperate.

He collected all the offerings into a clean yellow cloth, and went into the Knights' office. It felt like a transgression, poking about in the boss's desk drawers. Rows of Knight eyes burrowed into his back from the wall of family portraits behind the desk.

'You lot,' he turned on them. 'You can just bugger off. If you'd done your part of the work properly, we wouldn't be in this fix.'

He found a packet of chewing gum, forgotten behind a set of carefully ordered ledgers in the top drawer of the desk. That would help combat the attack of both cravings – the food and the nicotine – he thought, as he folded the first piece into his mouth.

He puffed up the stairs to the second floor, on a mission to hunt and gather. The spinning, twisting and finishing floors had been out of bounds for years because they were uninsured. The handle was cold and greasy to the touch as he eased open the heavy metal fire door. It clanged him into a place that stopped him dead just inside. Large baskets had been abandoned there full of bobbins and cones of yarn, their colours dulled by a furring of dust. The yarn was ready to be woven into sheets of cloth, but had never made the journey down to the floor below. On a windowsill, a faded ledger had been left open, scribbled with notes of orders and phone numbers of suppliers. The residue in a mug was veneered in mould, and a paperback lay open face down, never finished.

Light from the windows was blocked by the rows of twisting

frames; oil-blackened statues marching a funeral procession away to the far end of the hall, metallic edges softened by sticky dust. . The vast room was without movement or voice or life. But the spindles, the gears, the leather belts connecting the machines to the wheels of the overhead drive shafts – it was all supposed to turn and move.

When his father died, George had gone home to Yorkshire. He wanted to believe in his father's death, witness it himself. But the face 'at rest' in the curtained room had shocked him. He was sure he'd been shown to the wrong coffin.

'It's not him,' he'd protested, marching straight back to the funeral director's office.

'I'm sorry, sir.'

'Sorry?'

'People change. Even after just a few days. Without the breath in them.'

George stared at the man, trying to believe that the prostrate figure in there with the parchment face had been the man he called Da, who liked to down three pints of John Smiths every night at the Golden Fleece, who, after four, went red in the face and occasionally fluttered his fingers on the mouth-organ.

He spat out the ball of chewing gum which seemed to be making it hard to breathe, turned and walked away from the twisting machines. The door clashed shut, echoing behind him as he lurched back down the stairs. He lost heart, didn't venture to the top floor. He'd never been keen on it anyway. The last time he'd had to go up to get something, he'd found greasy water pooling on the floorboards, rusty machines, and had felt the whole building shudder and sigh up there under the high roof. It had reminded him of a dark plantation of too-close spruce trees he'd once walked through, whose straight bare trunks above him swayed and sang against each other like untuned violins.

He couldn't help thinking, as he got back to Madonna singing about prayers on the little transistor, that if it wasn't for him, the weaving floor would soon be inert too. The thought weakened his defences, allowing the craving to sink its teeth in further, urging him to pound down the stairs, unlock the door, and march out of the gate with the cigarette in his mouth, the strike ready. He needed that comfort, blast and bugger it. But if he left the building now, he'd likely never get back in.

The loom clamoured back into action, its business programmed by the wooden buttons that jumped their way around the belt to direct the pattern – the magical combination of vertical and horizontal that laid threads, meshing them into the subtle diagonals of tweed.

Once the loom was running smoothly, he wandered to the window, lifting a corner of the plastic sheeting that had been stapled over it to try and keep some heat in. The cost of proper double glazing had been a joke. Over the years he'd watched from here the posties' vans going past; the lady cycling to the Spar with a small dog in her front basket; the old boy with the bent back, passing on his constitutional every day at five to three. But people don't often think to look up, not unless they have a specific reason to do so.

He could see Rory the joiner still slumped in the driver's seat of the van with a newspaper. His hand flopped out of the open window holding a cigarette, needling George. Then he turned in his seat and looked directly up. They locked gazes for a moment without any gesture on either part, and then Rory turned back to his newspaper, and raised the hand with the cigarette to his mouth. His chest rose. And then fell.

Rory had come the day before too. There had been bangs on the door, followed by cries of, 'Open up, George! We're held up in our other jobs because of you.' Standing just behind it, George saw how the main door rattled against the bolt he had drawn across inside.

'Go ahead,' he'd shouted. 'Nail me in.' He turned and stomped back up to the first floor.

Before the phone had been cut off, he'd heard it ring a few times in the office. He answered it once, curious in case it was another order that he might fulfil from his solitary confinement.

'Knight and Co.,' he'd said.

'Don't be daft, George.'

'Hello, Nancy.'

'It's not Knight and Co. anymore now, is it?' she said softly.

'I've an order to finish.'

'What are you eating? I've made fish and chips.'

'It's the Glen Alder tweed.'

'George.' There had been a silence in which he thought he heard a tearful gulp. 'Where on earth are you sleeping?'

'No shortage of wool bales in here for bedding. I'm tough, like.'

'Not Indiana Jones though.' She tried to laugh. 'Your Last Crusade, is it?'

'More Nelson Mandela,' he said.

'You're making it your prison in there are you?'

He wanted to get on now, was ready to put the phone down, but she said, 'I phoned Jo.'

'Oh, aye.'

'He said you were a stubborn old fool.'

'What would he know?'

'He is your twin. He said the fish and chips would do it.'

'I'm not on hunger strike.' As he said it, the fish and chips swam across his vision for a second too long, trailing a gulp of saliva and a dull whine in his stomach.

'George,' she put on her negotiator's voice. 'They need to board the place up. I mean. You can't stay in there for ever. Our garden'll go to rack and ruin for one thing.'

He listened to a silence, the suggestion of a muffled sob at the end of the line.

'Are you trying to make yourself a martyr to the place?' she said.

Worn threads of memory tugged vaguely at him, the frayed ends of rumours from early in the century that reminded him he wouldn't be the Mill's first sacrifice. But he thought better of mentioning it. In fact he didn't wish to think of it, with the dark coming on, and him working alone as the man had been then, according to the stories. Some sort of strike-breaking, he seemed to remember, igniting a fever of anger, that left behind ashes and reek. 'Come on, love,' he said.

'What do you mean, "come on",' she shrieked. 'How could you do this to me?'

'No need to get your knickers in a twist, duck.'

He put the phone down. The next calls went unanswered and when he'd raised the receiver to his ear that morning, there had been no dialling tone anymore.

He calculated it would take another three hours to complete the length of tweed, if all went well, if there weren't too many broken threads to mend. He wouldn't be able to do the finishing or mill it properly, but at least the thing would be woven – his part complete.

He put his hand on the sheet of cloth inching with tiny jumps towards the roller at his knees, felt the thump, thump, thump vibrating through it, consoling and familiar. The length grew through the rhythmic, complex dance of the loom. It intrigued him how this had all grown out of the primitive hand loom and the hand-flicked flying shuttle, until the age of power enhanced it with speed and mechanised patterns. But it brought costs too. The number of people needed to run the weaving had staggered down and down with changes in fashion and technology, loss of tradition and competition from cheap factories elsewhere in the world, until now the bosses were prepared to let the whole damn thing go.

Back at the window he saw that the sky was darkening, the joiner had gone, presumably without boarding up the door. But now there was a single figure outside, an oval face straining upwards. Hands on hips. The lips were opening and closing and the hands coming up around the mouth. He pulled off his ear defenders but he couldn't so much hear as see the thin cry, 'George'. He saw her frantic beckonings, the stab of her finger towards the front door. It felt to him as if he was observing Nancy's attempts to communicate with someone standing just behind him. He could almost make out the dark mole that decorated her cheek, knew the hunch of her shoulders, the feet that had splayed unevenly as she'd aged. But he felt a distance of centuries between them. He let the plastic flap downwards, and went back to his work.

He would need to spend another night. He was getting tired now, dehydrated perhaps, without his usual mugs of dark sweet tea. He counted the jammy dodgers into piles, each representing a three-hour stretch. He could have the pork pie for his evening meal, the last sandwich for his breakfast. He'd drink half the Irn Bru tonight and save the rest for the morning. He was a survivor. He had a strategy. The tweed would get finished.

And then. Bang. The power went off. Lights out. Loom immobile. A rasping intake of breath. Silence.

He glared at the loom in the fading light. He went to the window, saw Nancy still standing there with her hands on her hips, looking at her feet now. He was ready to accuse her. Had she done this to him, colluding with that poofter in Edinburgh and the electric company?

A great weariness hovered and then sank onto his shoulders, pressing him down onto a stool, hands spread on his knees, head bowed. God, for a cigarette now. The craving had begun to have a colour – like the bluebell crossway that had been in action when the power went off, but a more electric version of it. Perhaps it was more like the acidic shades of lime and pink and whatnot that young Knight had bought in. He was going to call it the Greenham Tweed he said, something about celebrating the efforts of those lesbians chaining themselves to the fence to stop Cruise Missiles. He liked to think of it as 'the spirit of the 80's'.

Of course it had failed. George could have told him that most people were quite happy for the smelly women to stay chained up, and anyway it was traditional colours customers wanted, not that new garish stuff. The result? A storeroom full of wasted yarn. A lot of it was already wound onto pirns, ready to go in the shuttles, but had never got that far once they'd realised there was no demand.

Sickness gnawed at his stomach, and there was a drilling at his temples. The pitch of his craving and anger crashed together and seemed to pulse acidic colours in front of his eyes.

He thought of his twin brother, Jo, who'd been forced out of the trade in Yorkshire in much the same way almost a decade before, but had embraced a new life almost immediately. A militant-turned-salesman. Pathetic really, when you thought how he'd fought alongside the unions all his life and then backed off, got behind the wheel of a Metro and drove off in quite another direction with his air freshener dangling above his head.

Unions had never been a big deal at this mill. It was too small, too family-orientated, too lacking in the tradition of organisation and so far away from the rest of the industry, either in the Borders or in Yorkshire. But that didn't mean he hadn't stood up to things. And with a lifetime of it, another ten years on Jo, his old lopsided shoulders felt like the greased steel beams that held up the place, the industry. How could he give in to the bastards now?

But. No water. No power. A wife jumping up and down outside. Should he just pick up his snap-box, put on his hat, and make his last journey down the worn stone steps that had rung and clattered with so many feet in the past? Should he just open the great door, step out, and let it slam behind him?

A ship's captain stays on the bridge until the water washes over the very last thing, he thought – the top of his own cap. There was no water here, but there could be fire, at the graze of a match-head. The place would take nothing to go up, soaked as it was in a hundred and sixty years of lanolin and machine oil. Wasn't temptation pulling him anyway, towards that taboo cigarette? He could leave it to chance, just take no action if a spark from the ash happened to fall on the waiting yarn. He would watch, breathing a tempo with his cigarette, in and out. He took it from the packet again, placed it between his lips. This time he took out the box of matches too, with its own reassuring rattle.

He pictured a flame, running like a small creature along the top edge of the wooden shaft of the loom. It reached the end and then curled downwards along the vertical edge, met the warp threads stretched tight between rollers at front and back. He watched with fascination as the sombre warp sprang into a long taut sheet of colour, mesmerising in red, blue and yellow. It danced up into hungry flames, and started to billow black smoke towards the high ceiling.

Night was creeping in. He took a match from the box and pinched it between thumb and forefinger. Then he carefully replaced cigarette and match into their boxes. The tweed lay still, the length unfinished. He leant forward until his head met the edge of the loom. As his cheek grazed the rough yarn and his breath tickled to and fro through the raised hairs of the cheviot wool, he plunged deeply and unexpectedly into sleep.

In his brief dream, he was back in Yorkshire, sitting on a man's knee, his grandfather's probably, and they were together flicking the leather whip that sent the shuttle across the hand loom, first one way, then the other. The lazy schlick and schlock of the shuttle banged a soft slow rhythm.

When he woke up it was completely dark. He looked out of the window at an empty orange-lit street. He was the only boss now. He found a torch and went to the storeroom. He knew what he was going to do.

By the time he walked away from the loom with the unlit cigarette clamped in his mouth and a parcel under one arm, the dusk was falling on the following day, and his feet seemed to float above the steps rather than strike them. Each breath was marked by the bruised rise and fall of his ribs, and his shoulders and arms ached with the effort of his slow and laborious hand-work. He'd eaten the last jammy dodger three hours before.

As he unlocked and stepped out of the heavy front door, he

heard a car door slam.

'How're you doing, George?' It was Rory, the joiner, walking towards him with two planks under his arm, a hammer in his hand.

'Aye,' said George through tight lips.

'Had enough now?'

Rory slotted the planks into the brackets he had already fixed to either side of the door and put a hand in his nail belt.

George laid down the parcel and gestured for the hammer. He took a three-inch nail from Rory's hand, held it against the wood, and swung the hammer with his feeble remaining strength, willing himself to hit it square. Bang. It sank deep into the plank. Bang. Bang. Even when the head was virtually vanished under the frayed wood, he continued to swing until Rory nodded at him, put out his hand to take the hammer back, and finished the job.

George picked up the parcel and turned his back on the door, walking stiff, crooked, but what he thought of as stately steps, along the path and out of the gate. Once on the street, he paused and took the matches from his overall pocket. The strike flared its ribbon through the evening curtain of quiet and gloom. An intoxicating lightness seared through his body with the first breath. Perhaps it was the empty stomach, the days of abstinence, the old frame of his bones swaying towards dereliction, but the lightness swiftly cut away and sweat cooled his forehead instead, his bowels gripping tight in a message of nausea. He clutched the gate post, tried to find a hill, a horizon to steady his tipping gaze.

He clung to the parcel containing the pattern book with all the last knowledge and mystery of the Mill's weavers, and the last length of tweed. At one end the tweed matched the bracken and granite he saw now in the hills around him, speckled and subdued by the dusk. But at the other end, in a painful marathon of hand-thrown shuttles, he had woven the blaze of his farewell with its flaming clashes of purple, lemon yellow and pink. No-one would recognise it as tweed except himself.

He watched the ash accumulate at the cigarette tip and crumble onto asphalt, then knocked off the burning end, put it back in the packet for later. For when he had something in his stomach.

Steadied now, he pushed away from the gate post and fixed the Mill with burning eyes. Ranks of darkened windows. The bell tower sparring up brave at one end. But he noticed for the first time the triumphant buddleia straggling from it, its leaves and branches shadowing a smoky haze against the fading sky. It was now the tallest thing on the roof: the new crown.

He turned, started to limp towards home, the cool, damp evening air filling and emptying from his lungs. He could almost smell the fish and chips ahead.

Spring 1913

All in Good Time

I've that much to tell John when you finish with him tonight. About the meeting, and of course, the fire that's left its smell to mooch through Perth. But I can wait. Haven't I proved to the three of us already how I can wait? I've my wee rhymes to call to the crows. *One crow, sorrow, Two crows, mirth, Three, a wedding, Four, a birth.* Aye, I'm the expert at waiting alright. And this bench will give my poor tappitless legs a wee rest.

You're too solid for fire yourself, aren't you? You've those great lumbering stones hoiked out of the depths of the earth, and your hardy skeleton inside, and your rows of windows where you display workers, heads and arms bobbing in a rhythm with their machines. That's what you'd say, eh? You'd just say the pavilion was asking for it. What daftie of a building is made of wood? Might as well build with paper.

I've brought John the headline to see: 'DISASTROUS FIRE IN PERTH'. And a photograph, look. Just a few embers left to kick about. They say it was the women. The wee message for Maister Asquith has been put it in the newspaper: 'Justice before cricket; let a democratic government play the game.' Aye, if he came here, he'd be for a warm welcome, right enough. Right up his bahoochie.

And I've to tell John too about Miss Parker and Miss Christie, coming all the way from Dundee to speak, and then having to thole the wrath of the Perth folk for their precious cricket pavilion. Look how my coat cuff's torn and frayed. I got pulled and shoved that much by the crowd. And the words hurled at the Misses from men's mouths. I couldn't hear a word of their speeches. I just caught the bit about how we won't change things with lady-like meetings anymore.

What I learnt today is it's 'deeds not words'. From now on we're not to let ladies in London and Dundee weave schemes for us, we've to get stuck in ourselves, wherever we are. Wherever, do you hear?

And so. Look! How I've handbills to take to all the cottages, a big pile of them. And posters. Maybe I'll find some village lassies to lend a hand. There's the women who had the jumble sale, but they look at me toff-like, because I'm new here I suppose, and I'll bet they're agin the WSPU tactics.

John would help me. 'The Trades Unions'll be stronger if women get the vote,' he aye says. He would help me, but that you're keeping him so busy.

I was that glad to get on a train out of town. That's new for me, eh? I changed trains, and then took the trap over the goat track. It's slow as pouring treacle. Who would think we'd let a hill lead us such a dance? Up the way, wriggling round all those bends, and then all that way down before you're back into the glen here. In a hundred years they'll have found a way to travel more direct, to shunt these wretched mountains out the road.

When John looks up at that hill, what he sees is a landmark. He says once the point of it's dead central, an even slope on each side, then he knows he's home. It's not the same hill at all from the other side – it's got a long sharp ridge like John's letter-knife. You can't trust something that can alter its shape like that.

The grass was yellow-dead up there. But the bark of the birches was all red and purple, like it was roaring at you, what with the sunshine. You could feel the life jostling just under the rock and soil. I found it all a wee bit breathy. The sun. And us being all peely-wally after the winter. Like a wee flame growing till it beats. Like, wheesht, that moment I get with John. Aye, that moment. You know what I'm talking about.

Five brings silver, Six takes wealth, Seven crows a secret, More I cannae tell.

'An honest living for country folk,' he aye says about your work. 'It's that simple.'

But I'm not so sure. When he talks about the sales to Australia and America, he gets excitable. It seems like profit's what it's all about. And who gets the profit? Aye, Maister Greasy-Forelock-Knight, and the son that's picking up the reins from him.

'Why put all your heart into someone else's venture?' That's what I says to John.

Nine, Ten, Eleven, Twelve.

Anyways, I'm on the road to my own vocation. I can stop fashing about his.

'All in good time,' he said, when he read the letter.

He's my sensible man, so he is. He says there's no rush while we're getting settled in here. We've no great need for more money right now. But I'll be starting soon. Once we're settled. And he'll dance his signature across the page to back me up. And then you'll miss our wee blethers, eh?

Thirteen, Fourteen, Fifteen, Sixteen, so many heads you've never seen.

Come on my rough-faced friend. I'm alone but for your crabby face. You don't have much to say for yourself, eh?

The shift must end soon.

Let him go.

A mill that sleeps at night like a wean. Who ever heard of it? There's no light at your windows, no hullarackit from a night shift. You're just a sonsie hound, no even flicking an eye to watch me slip past. You wee deefie. Am I right, or am I wrong?

I could sleep on the edge of a razor myself. But someone's got to do it. Like I told you, it's deeds not words now. It's for all the lassies of tomorrow. Aye, and they'll be glad of me, you'll see.

Wheesht! Don't tell. You've no seen me with this roll of posters and a pot of glue. Aye, I've one for the post-box mouth, and one for the church door. And I've one more, right enough. A spare. You've a face like a wet Monday. We'll change that for you, eh?

Don't screech so, gate. Shh. Perhaps you'll hear me now, eh? With the jiggle of matches in my pocket. There by habit. I should have left them on the shelf.

Door, flat and smooth. A slap of glue. And there you are, with a wee decoration. Purple, white and green, you'll shine out in the daylight. 'Votes for Women', you'll cry.

Eech! What's that? Nothing, nothing. How the smallest things ambush me when I'm in the dark, trying not to be seen. A branch rubbing against another, a shadow on the wall. And here's a night frost come to nibble at me, giving me the shivers.

Don't clype. We're pals, mind. Right?

So what is it you'll entertain me with the day? Nothing? More of the same of your churning machines and nodding heads? At least some days there's distraction while I wait.

I look at the hills, right enough. There was that tree, stood up there on its own like the capitalist mannie does, came crashing down in the January gales. And yet that group standing together there. Did they fall? Like hell. They held each other up. That's what women are like when they're together. We'll force the men to change, just by keeping still. You'll see.

Old Maister Knight sat beside me on this very bench yesterday. All as if we were pals. The picture of politeness he was. He sent a wee procession of men up that hill, each with a different length of tweed to hold up. You should have heard the humming and hawing while he looked through his glasses.

He asked me, 'Of the eight, which is best?'

All as if I cared. As if that was what I came to sit here for. As if he hasn't heard they cry me 'the crabbit wifie'.

And though it skittered across my mind not to answer at all, but to say something else like 'You want to speak to me, you share your wealth with the folk that earns it for you' … though I thought to say that, I told him that I saw just seven.

'Aha,' he cried and passed me the glasses to find the eighth, which I only found because the man had been on the swally. His cheeks were bright red against the stubby dark heather and the birches.

'That's a rare piece of magic,' I told him, 'how that man disappeared.'

The old goat winked at me and said how I'd better watch out for my John. Aye, I thought, you're not wrong there. Then he was up and bellowing on his whistle for them to come down again, after a wee bob and bow to myself, and back inside your clanking door, his decision made.

My John showed me the vanishing cloth at home once, the tweeds you make in there for the estates. I can barely see a stitch in them. It's like they're hewn rather than woven, or grown like heather. He showed me the warp and the weft, one up the way, and one across. Three colours crossing a dull background. But it's that clever, the way it makes a diagonal that doesn't follow either the warp or the weft. And he told me how the tweed's designed to fracture a person somehow, breaking them into tiny pieces so they vanish against that big beast of a hoary hill.

I know the look of the hills now, from gawping at them every day in place of the Clyde or Glasgow Green. I've become quite the expert at looking. I find in the tweed the red of the bracken when it dies back, and the faint strip of a bluebell field, and a mottle of green with the same look as when the sun shines on a forest. And it gives me a wee bit shiver to think about making people blend into it like that. All as if they're rotting.

But what I've learnt now is why they want to vanish. Those boys on the estates, they want to look like that lump of a hill up there in their caps and jackets and gaiters, so they can creep up on the deer and rabbits with their guns. And that's not all. I've heard there's talk of uniforms, a bid going in for the khaki and the blues. Another disguise. That's what you're about my cruel cold friend, is it not? Killing.

So this is country ways.

And now John says there's no need for me to sit out here waiting for him. Nor sitting at the kitchen table reading pamphlets. Nor travelling to rallies every week. There's work to do, he says.

My husband. He's turned himself countryman.

Once you've done with him, nights, he's out behind the house in the gloaming, digging away at the soil. Aye, you should see the sweat glistening on his arms. And he has me weeding between the tatties and the carrots and the round-head cabbages which he says will last us through the winter. If I didn't know him so, I'd think all these things are to harness me to the house and the land.

Then he brought home chickens. Aye, chickens! I'm the one has to chase them into their house before night. I can't help but let the shrieking come out of me, to mimic theirs. Their russet feathers flounce up behind them, and I jig around them, shooing and flicking my apron. I told him it's like his mother, trying to shoo me to be a proper wife, and get with child. The corner of his mouth lifts in the chitter of a smile, but he's still for sending me off with the warm eggs for her. I carry them there in a basket, tickled by the odd feather, when he goes off to you in the mornings. I ask him, you're not shooing at me yourself, are you? Because it's not a hen-house where I want to go.

And now it's a cow. He's so grand and pleased with himself and doing so well, thanks to yourself and your Maister Knight, sir. An animal to go in the back-yard, he says. And he wants to pay a boy to lead it down to the river for the grazing. It's a good investment. And I can turn the milk into butter and cheese for us, so I can, according to himself!

'Is that what you want of your wife?' I tease him. 'Is it that you're wanting me for. The muscle in my arms, rather than my fine ideas?' And I remind him then about the letter that's waiting. 'Don't forget,' I tell him. 'I'll be away for that nurse training before too long once you've put your hand to the pen, given your wife "permission". I'll be making my own career. And then who will turn the butter?'

Think you're big, the day, do you? Aye. Flashing your windows in the sun like sequins on some gaudy gown, and turning your strange stone all silver and glistering of a sudden to sook in a big crowd of onlookers. It's like you've shrugged your shoulders and sent all those winter crows spraying back into the branches where they belong. Shoulders tall. Yourself. Quite the centre of things, eh?

But a wee coat'll fit you.

Look at they weans staring all clarty-faced, and there's more, quite a crowd, come out the cottages to gawp.

But what were you thinking of, you and Maister Knight, dragging workers in, when they should be parading in town for May Day? That's where I should be. I would have gone, but John said he'd to be here for the deliveries, being the Big Man now.

I mind last year, the procession we made with the brass and the pipe band through Trongate and Saltmarket. All the associations were out together – the Clarion Cycle Club and the National League of Blind Workers. Then being in that great crowd, twenty thousand they said on Glasgow Green, and how we proclaimed May 1st should be a holiday for all. All like one big family, so we were. You've no idea. The banners parading, and the wee platforms with speakers for this and that, and speeches in Yiddish and Russian, and Maister French calling for a 'right, red, revolution', and Miss Sylvia Pankhurst herself up there, saying that the cooperative commonwealth will only happen if women as well as men manage it.

It was shoulder to shoulder, smiles sparking as we caught the eye of the next person. The flap and beat of the words on the banners, and the shouts and songs thrown into the air. And I felt tears rising, and the joy of knowing that we all believed in the same and were proud to march side by side. And I knew then that my life darning my brothers' socks was behind me, and all was ahead, all freedom was coming in my life together with John. And I wouldn't write any more to Da, and answer his questions about making myself into a wee wife with the baking and so on. I felt like writing to him to say I know now where my true family is.

And you keep us away from all that, from our brothers and sisters? It hurts just like the time I burnt my hand on the stove, a teasing scald, to think what I'm missing.

Aye. You've to concentrate now. Oh, there's plenty noise for the occasion. Listen to that cable on the hoist, creaking with the lump of machine it's hauling up. And there's the men. Hands on hips, anxious, watching their precious fittings past the ground floor windows. Brand new power looms, my dearie, the fancy Dobcross ones. It's a wonder to me, how your floor will thole the stamping wild dance, once the looms are all a-going, with all that lumpen weight jostling and jumping.

John says you were all working in the dark ages. And now? You'll be the new-fangled thing, eh? Aye, you'll be as fast as the batter of my tongue. To cope with the new demand, the expansion, with your night shifts starting, and new workers being bussed in from other villages, making up for the families away to their new lives in Canada.

I asked him, and I slid a wee needle into my voice, I couldn't help it. I asked him how many looms they'll be minding now, with this new efficiency. Will it become two, when no-one's looking?

They've left from Stanley too I've heard. An exodus. I wonder what it is they go to in Canada. Those adverts say, 'Domestic servants guaranteed good wages in good homes'. Mind to take your stockings and cutlery, but. There's none there.

And there he is. My man. Look how his hair's flopping over his eyes these days. Annie, my old Neilston pal, would never believe it. A Union man no more. Maister Foreman. Overseeing it all from the first-floor goods door. Proud of him, are you, stood with his hand pressed on your wall, waiting for his precious machines to rise up to him?

'We can live well now,' he said to me. 'Go and get yourself a new dress.' As if that's what it is I want.

John's leaning out, grappling with the warp beam that's swinging level with him. So many eyes are on you today, and on him. A Spring day, so's we can bask as we watch. The village folk gathered, but not one of them's a friendly word for me. Why did my man bring me here? I'm like a flower grown from a seed that's blown in from foreign parts.

You've been busying him too much. In my pocket, under the box of matches, there's the tattered edge of the letter. I found it under a pile of papers on his desk, still unsigned. Overlooked.

'Left it there to think on,' so he says.

Now he's thought long enough. He's got his position. Now I need mine, my nurse training. It's time to get started. You send him home these days with his hair limp and greasy. He smells of machine oil and lanolin, and his face is slippy in my hands, not sandstone-rough. I've seen what you're making him into.

So don't you ground him with your loom weights.

I want him out here.

Then I'll make sure the pen doesn't slip from his hand, no till he's given me that signature.

2003

The Lost Son

It was as if Mr Mzee's words had propelled James Knight into that twenty-four-hour journey – into a relay of road and air and rail. Their *tête a tête* at the Ministry of Culture, Women and Youth, with a fan gusting at the loose edges of paper, and the sounds of the street rising with dust through the shutters, spun him into an inevitable trajectory. He felt like a small boy again, packed off to boarding school by his parents, knowing that attempts at resistance would be futile.

'The project is underway. Much has been done in your two years here. It has been a great honour to have you amongst us. And now,' Mr Mzee drew breath as if something precious was to follow. 'It is time for you to go back to your family, Mr Juma. They must need you too.'

James replied quickly, 'But I was thinking I could stay another year.'

Mr Mzee laughed. 'We all long to be with our families, to be in our homeland. I remember this for myself, when I was in Germany.'

James tried again. 'You don't think that with another year

we'd have the training sorted?' He heard the bluster in his voice, the need to convince. 'The men can do the heddle-making, warping, beaming, threading of shafts and the reed, everything for the weaving. But they need to be able to do a bit of loom maintenance.'

The anticipation of the journey arrived in his body like the shivery grip of a fever. He grasped at slices of the day through the office shutters. A line of women wrapped in *khangas* processed like a string of bright beads along the road. A basket on the back of a bicycle was ornamented with the forked tail of a yellow-finned tuna. Vespas smoked by, the riders wearing builders' helmets to comply faint-heartedly with the law. Dust rose.

The sensations slid away from him as he imagined his feet cooling on the plane, the food delivered in plastic trays and sanitised to Western tastes, without the rich addition of coconut milk or ants in the flour. It was usually hard to visualise from the embracing heat here, but a sudden picture came of Scotland – one of those dense still days when the tops of trees are bitten off by cloud, and the sheep, stone walls, and sky reflect only shades of white. He imagined rain sheeting onto dark roads; headlights and spray; faceless transport. No one noticing him.

He couldn't even identify where home was now. Not his flat in Edinburgh, rented out – why would he live in the ferocious wind-bite of that city again anyway? Then it came, as if he had been keeping it from himself. It would have to be his parents' house in Perth, at least to start with. He pictured them tucking a hand under each of his elbows on the railway platform, and marching him away for interrogation as his feet scrabbled and pawed to hold their ground. 'Did it go wrong there too?' they would ask. And who would contradict them, tell them how he had started something here which might just flourish?

No-one at home could know what it meant to witness Mohammed's face when the first cloth had rolled towards him onto the beam. As the smile had sprung his features into life, the rest of the men in the workshop crept forward, congregating around his loom, looking between his face and the cloth, edging into laughter almost as if they had witnessed a miracle. Mohammed continued to build the cloth, bouncing back the reed to consolidate the fabric, finding his rhythm. Soon all the looms were going, and the workshop had filled with the regular soft thud of the shafts rising and falling, the reeds bashing and shuttles shimmying to and fro. Light would band in between gaps in the latticed walls of the hut. With it came the sounds of children playing under the shelter of palms outside. The workshop had come to feel like James's own place.

Not prepared to lose the agenda wholly to Mr Mzee, he grappled on: 'I have some more ideas for business development, you see.'

'You have given us many ideas. So very many ideas.'

'Thank you. I'd like to see if we can tap into the Mombasa market – there are plenty of tourists there with money to spare.'

'Mr Juma. Please join us for sodas and *sambusas*. We are so happy to invite you – myself and Mr Makame. When will you come for a celebration?'

James saw that he was not being offered an option – he was being offered a leaving party. From his preparation for this posting he knew that he was only there to train people, to build capacity, that he should make himself dispensable. And yet and yet and yet. Everyone in the workshop still deferred every small decision to him. They had adapted his name to something familiar to them – 'Juma' – and invited him to meet their families. They laid out before him plates of breads, fish, meats, even biryani or pilau as a mark of occasion. Strangers called out his name in the street.

Cloth was not only rolling off the looms, it was for sale in the little tourist shops in the Stone Town, with labels attached in dollars. A quality product from organic cotton, hand-dyed. He'd even seen tourists on the beach with it draped and wound over their bikinis.

He was proud himself to wrap a Kinyonga-brand *kikoi* around his waist each morning when he got up to stretch on the step of his house and go to the stall for bread and bananas. In the way of local fishermen he wore nothing underneath. It reminded him of wearing the kilt. But the slim length of the *kikoi* from waist to ankle made him feel sinuous, even, dare he admit to it, sexy.

They had talked about producing *kikois* impregnated with pesticides in the same way as mosquito nets. They might even have got money from aid programmes to do it. But that was another project that hadn't yet been realised, and he for one would only sit outside at night if he was wearing long trousers, socks and full-length sleeves, armoured against the squadrons of mosquitoes that whined after his blood.

Mr Mzee was spreading the fingers of both his hands on the desk and smiling at him. 'Your obligation is not to us. Now, please allow us to celebrate what you have done for us. Can we depend on you, Mr Juma?'

He looked through the shutters beyond Mr Mzee and recalled his own words when the inevitable redundancies had come at home, thirteen years before. 'It's harsh, but it's economic reality,' he'd said to the men. 'I'm so sorry, but the market has collapsed. There's nothing more that Knights can do.'

They'd surely seen it coming anyway in the dwindling use of the Mill building – three floors closed up, until finally just the first-floor looms remained. Plastic sheeting was stapled at the windows, keeping in the meagre heat and gas fumes seeped out by the Super Ser. At the end, George Kaye, bolshy and squint-shouldered, had shut himself in there to make a point, to complete his last length of tweed. He was so engrained in tradition he couldn't grasp the opportunity for change, take the redundancy money and run with it.

'It's the facts of life, George,' he'd said. 'You have to build a different future. Not one that revolves around this monument beckoning you to it every morning.'

When he told each of the men, he had felt behind him the presence of his father, his grandfather, and all the 'greats' who had built the woollen business up, deftly responding to this pressure or that, diversifying into ready-mades when the market required it, always innovating, and coming up with benefactor's schemes for the workers – smallpox inoculations, life insurance, savings schemes. Always encouraging self-reliance. And it had been his accident of birth to inherit something that ailed, causing people to say things had been different in his father's time, that this was young blood turned bad, wrecking the lives of whole families.

As the Mill went dark, its windows offering themselves up to be smashed by flying stones, its roof slates slipping, the patriarchs all lined up to inspect James when he lay in bed at night, asking, 'Are you sure you've done all you can? What about making it into a museum?' Even after ten years in Edinburgh, they returned to ask, 'Why are you running away? Africa!' And the whispers: 'Couldn't even keep a wife. She ran off.' The unuttered implication being that they didn't blame her.

Hadn't his parents sent him away to school at the age of nine for the very purpose of preparing him for a life of difficult decisions on behalf of others? Had there been an inkling that he wasn't up to it even then, when he was extracted from the regiment of boys in knee-length grey shorts to spend weekends at home? His father would take him to the Mill office and peer at him from behind stacks of enormous pattern books on his high dark desk. The patriarchs watched from the wall behind his father's head. He was brought there, he realised now, to be taken into manly confidences, to start fitting into his future business environment. But his feet didn't touch the ground from the leather armchair and he usually sat on the floor.

When his own photograph was added to the wall, after university, there appeared to be no resemblance to the other portraits. Nervousness hovered behind the eyes and he wasn't even wearing a tie.

He succumbed to the leaving party. 'Of course,' he said to Mr Mzee. 'Thank you.'

The Ministry car came to take him to the airport in the early evening. At the time he had applauded the building of the new road that allowed goods to get from village to town in little more than an hour. But the car moved too quickly for him now, and he clutched at cameos flashing through the glass, cramming them into his memory as if into pockets from where they could be unfolded to view later.

It was his favourite time of day, when the low sun laid palm trunks in striped shadows across the road and people congregated in a kind of carnival on every village verge, moving through a hazy light smoked up by the braziers lit for the night ahead. Street stalls displayed lines of coconuts, limes, oranges. In one shop, a man lay flat on the empty counter, head back in the abandon of sleep. Over-amplified radios crackled out the news. Ahead of the car, crossing the road, chickens were pressed tail high into undignified strides to avoid being run over. There were ox carts and streams of schoolchildren returning home to swerve around. An open truck was full of singing footballers.

He gazed out at the adobe houses which had been sliced in half by the new road, leaving the fronts sheared off like dolls' houses. The occupiers had just moved uphill of the development, living on in the unaffected rooms.

'Were they paid compensation?' he asked.

The driver laughed, not apparently seeing any need for a serious answer.

James was seen off at the airport – seen off in both senses, he felt. There were sincere handshakes, a gift of cake, egg-rich and greasy in a plastic bag, and mangoes in a woven banana-leaf pouch. He accepted Mr Mzee's handshake without being able to meet his eyes. Then he was going through security where officials whispered his name coyly, and was watched until he reached the small departure lounge from where there was no return, to drink instant tea and join groups of Italians in short skirts and spaghetti-strap tops for the last chance to buy tourist tat. On their twenty-minute flight to the mainland they would barely reach 3,000 feet, crossing the turquoise gap between island and mainland, where reefs brushed the water's surface from below.

Amongst the rayon sarongs from Indonesia and the T-shirts promising in words across their fronts *Hakuna Matata* – 'no problems' here – he looked for 'his' products in the shop. He posed as an ordinary tourist as he ran his hand over the soft cotton, eavesdropping on what was said about colour and quality by the people in shuffling sandals around him. It was a habit, but meaningless now. 'Cotton!' the voices waiting at home said. 'What a betrayal.'

He sat down, still in Zanzibar, but moving into that tenuous international zone, becoming anonymous, his skin cooling in the air conditioning. Looking out through a wall of glass, fluorescent-jacketed men crawled over the small planes, feeding in suitcases and rucksacks, just as they would at another airport tomorrow morning. He thought about the miraculous deepening of colour just after sunset. Just before people became silhouettes against a pale night sky, their clothes and skin would escape the blanching effect of the sun and radiate dense saturated red and brown and gold.

Two years living without a TV, and the images he watched blearily on a version of the week's BBC World News made him flinch against his seatbelt and pull down the eye mask. Rows of faceless young men in desert uniforms. Wildly gesticulating people in streets of rubble. Flags and coffins carried on uniformed shoulders. Members of a British family comforting each other on a suburban sofa, and accusing the regiment of not providing the right kind of protective clothing. But it was the flattened streets of Basra that really got to him.

James remembered his father talking once about the bombings in Clydeside where he had gone with his own father to visit their affiliate company during the war. Dawn broke, the all-clear sounded, and people emerged from their shelters into a smashed and burning town. James's grandfather had apparently become heady and lost his sense of direction because of the sudden absence of the Singer Factory. One minute there was the familiar bulk of stone and steel, dominating the skyline and the economy. The next, gone. Blasted away. At Auchentoshan Distillery a warehouse full of whisky was set ablaze. James's father told him how he had been mesmerised by the inferno, as whisky poured into the nearby burn and created a finger of fire that pointed to the Clyde.

His father spoke of the devastation as if it were a shift in the mental as well as the physical landscape – almost like a liberation. It would be like removing Schiehallion from the Perthshire skyline, he'd said, the feeling of disorientation and desertion by an icon. It was also a release from a dominant influence – like the end of a long year at school. But this talk had been the result of an afternoon ripened by whisky, the words whispered almost guiltily. His father had seemed momentarily more human, but James hadn't seen that side of him since.

Suspended over the Sudanese desert, snatches of sleep came. He supposed it was sleep. He climbed a ladder propped against the crumbling wall of a building. On the other side of its windows were expectant faces wanting something from him. But the windows were stuck fast, and none of the attachments on his Swiss Army Knife made any difference and there was a fire growing beneath him. He fell, waking, into his seat and sunrise over the Alps. Snow-sculpted peaks poked through cloud, inviting him to ski in the postcard sunshine before the inevitable drop into the bumpy cloud above Schiphol.

On the flight to Glasgow, he looked at his hands. The skin looked dry and wrinkled without the normal sheen of humidity. They were thinner too, more knobbly, as if they belonged to someone else. And already in this climate, his back had stiffened – he'd lost the loose feeling in his body; aged overnight.

A drum-beat of protestations had gathered in his head, a subconscious preparation, a defence. It must have been his father's war-time stories, thoughts of his grandfather and company history. The Mill had flourished at the signs of the

First War, with a sudden demand for khaki, navy blue, puttees. His grandfather had felt compelled to respond to the new market, despite the family's aversion to war. And wasn't that the beginning of the moral decay which bequeathed to James an undermined business that only needed a few shoves from cheap competition or some other hostile force to completely topple? So he inherited decline and redundancies and in turn had been blamed for it, for something which had deeper roots.

'Give me a break.' The drum-beat banged on and on. 'It wasn't my fault.'

He changed the money in his wallet to Sterling. He changed the Sim card in his phone. He got a bus into town. And finally, he got on a train to Perth.

He was dishevelled, unshaven, still in flip-flops when his parents would expect brown brogues. He had found a warm jacket, now pungent with mould after lying in the corner of a cupboard for two rainy seasons. He clung to the familiar smell and to his small bottle of Kilimanjaro water, still half full. He sipped it slowly, not wanting to finish it, as if such slight threads would keep him umbilically attached to another place.

The man sitting opposite was smiling and cradling a Debenhams bag in his lap. He hadn't flinched when James opened *The Guardian*. His glazed look made James wonder if he was already drunk even though it was only ten in the morning. Was he the kind of man who promises you're his best pal and pours his reeking breath over you? But there was no smell coming from him. James dropped his face towards the job adverts, lifted the paper slightly.

'Nice day,' the man said, storming through James's paper wall.

James looked up and out of the window, as if for the first time. As they moved into the countryside, the April day showed signs of Spring. Daffodils were pooled on garden lawns, and gorse beamed in clumps from hillsides, for all the world as if the sun had some heat in it. There was even some blossom in the trees and you could see people out in their gardens in T-shirts. There was so much grass here. So much green. And between trees he saw the slate shading which could only be the first shoots of a bluebell field.

'Going far?' The man was smiling at him now.

Jobs for EFL teachers in Poland were pulling James's eyes back downwards. Could he retrain as an English teacher? Maybe he should have gone straight to Poland, not even bothered reporting back, just to disappoint the family once more. He dragged his eyes back up to the man's face. 'Just to Perth.'

'Me too. Went down early this morning.' He crackled the bag against his chest. 'Had to get this.'

James had the corner of the newspaper in one hand, ready to turn the page. Pursue the conversation with this man now and he might as well give in, fold up his paper. Should he explain his fragile state after the long journey, his disorientation, his need for over-the-shoulder glances lest he forget where he'd come from? Should he plead to be left alone? He wasn't really in a fit state to have a conversation with a stranger hugging a bag.

The man's hair was sandy, his eyes watery, his hands trembling slightly. Looking at him more carefully, James saw the suggestion of a shiver in one corner of his mouth, but it looked less like drunkenness now. When James caught his glance, he was unable to resist the naked openness of the eyes, a sense of personal light emanating from the man. He sat back, disturbed.

The man laid the bag on the table between them, and opened it, lifting out a tissue-wrapped, beribboned parcel which he slowly and carefully opened. Something black nestled inside.

The man held up a dress, a finger hooked through each shoulder. It hung between them, concealing the man. James wiped a hand across his face.

A reflex made him touch the fabric. He knew it instantly. Viscose. Polyester lining in a gold colour. The dress concertinaed a fold at a time back into the tissue paper, revealing the man again. He carefully rewrapped it, and tied the ribbons.

'They didn't have it in the Debenhams in Perth,' he said.

James stared at him. The night had been too long.

'It had to be this one, see. This particular one.'

James remained pinned in his seat, paralysed. He wanted to carry on thinking about his normal breakfast-time back at the village, how he would be watering the passion-fruit vine which scrambled up from the *baraza*, squeezing lime juice onto papaya, biting into the yeasty *maandazi*, and drinking hot sweet tea. He would make the short cycle ride to the workshop, hearing with pleasure as he approached, the shafts already rising and falling – the rhythmic softness of hand looms.

'I see,' he managed.

'She phoned the Glasgow branch last night. They said they'd keep her back a size ten.' He spoke softly, as if emphasising some tenderness in the act, and then added more quietly. 'I said I'd come. Not working myself, at the moment.'

'She – your wife?'

'Daughter.' The man stroked a flat hand over the tissue paper and then slid it back into the carrier bag. He left it now on the table between them. 'She needs a bit of love and support right now.' The damp-eyed look had returned.

James nodded.

'It's for his funeral.'

Any sense James's numb mind had gained from this

conversation so far was now rattling away from him. 'Whose?' he asked.

'Her husband's. On Friday.'

James spoke quietly. 'I'm sorry.'

The man broadened his gentle smile and looked out of the window. James became suddenly afraid that the slight shiver in his cheek, the wet eyes, would erupt into something more, and embarrass them both.

'It's a fine dress,' James said. What would have come naturally in the Swahili language was, '*Atapendeza*' – literally, 'she will please', or be beautiful. Instead he had to settle for, 'She'll be proud to wear it, I'm sure.'

'You heard?' The man pinned a swift glance on him and then eased it away. 'I shouldn't be surprised, I suppose. It's been in all the papers.'

James wondered what 'it' was, and blustered towards comprehension. 'I've been out of the country. I haven't been reading papers really.'

'He was in the Black Watch.'

BBC images from the flight flashed up at him. So that was it. That explained the man's giddy state, the heightened value he gave a bit of cheap viscose which had been cut on a press with a hundred others and stitched together in an automatic frenzy of pumping needles. James guessed that the man had told his story to the shop assistants too. He would have been happy to wait while they scurried to another department for pink tissue paper and ribbons. They probably found him a chair, a cup of tea. He was, after all, shimmering today.

James noticed a middle-aged woman look over at their table from above her book. Even the schoolgirl with the black rimmed eyes seemed to be listening, as she chewed. The whole carriage seemed to have fallen into a respectful silence so that the swish of air against the windows, the rhythm of the rail joints, the opening and closing of the automatic door as the carriage rocked, all became amplified. It was as if the man had possession of some mysterious knowledge that they all wanted to brush against.

They were descending now, the train channelled between high stone walls – the final stretch before Perth. James knew from past times that people would start to collect their belongings and gather the thoughts that had strayed up sidings or branch lines. They would prepare, with combs and lipsticks, to present themselves to loved ones on the platform. They entered a tunnel and James saw in the window reflection that the made-up teenager was punching in her final text. With a jangle, the drinks trolley was lined up in the lobby ready to exit. Suddenly aware of the end of his long journey, the beginning of his new life, James wanted to know more.

'I heard there was a stooshie, whether their gear was up to it, up to what they were doing.'

The tunnel released them to sunlit warehouses. Two children bounced on a trampoline in a garden.

The man huffed softly, raised his eyebrows. 'Some are accusing.'

'Not you? Your daughter?'

'It's not about blame. It's what happened. We're concentrating on those that are left. Sticking together.' The man seemed to register the beginning of the pink brickwork of the station, the white picket fence marking familiarity, and pulled the carrier bag towards him.

But his last words were still thudding softly in James's fuddled mind. They echoed within some un-named place that felt hollow and distant.

'It was good to talk to you,' the man said, looking at him again, smiling.

James had barely slept. Hunger was gnawing at his stomach, and he was off-balance after the tumbled hours of dark and daylight. His bare toes were white with cold. He saw that the man meant what he said – even though James hadn't mentioned a job or a business or a hobby.

Something surged up in him and pulled him to his feet. The man stood up on the other side of the table. As James grasped the offered hand, he covered his right forearm with his left hand in the sincere, respectful Zanzibari style. His own eyes became watery. He would have hugged the man, but there was a table between them. And he was Scottish.

And that's how he was standing when the train soothed under the vaulted glass ceiling and against the platform. He saw his mother and father, grey and waiting side by side, his father leaning heavily on a stick. They looked like cornered animals, unmoving, whilst figures passed in front of them. Their hands fluttered, patting at each other and pointing as they caught sight of him.

Impelled out into the cool air, he dropped his bags onto the platform. Children leapt to hug relatives, and clung to careering trolleys. A spaniel raced between legs dragging a lead behind it. He was amongst smiling faces and spring clothes in red and blue and purple illuminated through the moss-covered skylights.

James stood with his arms at his sides, everything stripped away by the journey and watched his parents hobble towards him in a decrepit three-legged race, his father's face twitching between spasms of arthritic pain, his mother's hand gripped knuckle-white around her husband's elbow. They seemed an aged version of themselves after only two years. And yet, as he watched their approach, sparks of sudden recognition exposed his own eyes in his mother's face; the slight hook of his nose in his father's. His mother's mouth seemed twisted around something but he noticed that a red scarf brightened her neck, signalling a special occasion. He felt a flush rise in his own face as if in correspondence with it, and a wall of resistance crumbling away to reshape his horizon.

They drew towards each other, stretching across the distance of a few paces with tremulous smiles and half-extended arms. His parents limped into his embrace. James's bony knuckles, strong arms, and broad back built a fence around them. He felt their hands patting at his back.

'Good journey, son?' his father asked.

'Not so bad.'

'Your mother's got a salmon in for lunch, haven't you, dear?'

'I hope you're hungry,' she said.

They stayed, rocked by gusts from passing passengers and the suck of the train pulling out again, until the platform was quiet. Then James picked up his bags, and they walked together through the dark tunnel out onto the station esplanade. They waited, squinting out from a pool of sunlight that splashed against glass and lawn and blossom, for a taxi that would take them home.

October 1913

Traitor

Aye, I'm back after all those weeks. You missed me, eh? It's you I'm talking to, you lumbering fat-faced thing.

Anyway, here I am.

Aye, they found out I was married. Think that's a rare jest, do you? Some clype got word to the toffs and they gave me my jotters, out the door. I'll bet it was someone in the village, seeing me clambering on and off that trap so early in the mornings.

All I've to do is sit and stare at you again.

It's true I'll not miss it. Not the long lurching journey between glens, the hours it took to get to Strathearn. Not the scurrying to the dark corners of that big empty house, and all the silver to polish. Nor the domestic uniform – the badge to show you're manacled to Edinburgh folk while they're in their country residence.

But at least there was Dorothy, the other maid there – we'd talk long into the night about the women's struggle, and demonstrations we'd been on, and banners we'd make, and the words we'd put on them, when I shared her bed on the nights I didn't come home. A common spirit. It minded me of being with Annie and the lassies. Of my life before I was married.

John said why was it I wanted to go and work at the big house. 'Why? We're fine now I'm a foreman. We're not short of money. There's no need for you to work,' he said.

So I told him not to fash himself, I'd use my maiden name. They'd never know at the Mill, Maister Knight and that. And I looked him in the eye and said surely he believed like me this was my right, to work? And he sighed and shrugged. It was his wee concession to me. I could work away somewhere, in service, if I must.

I never thought he'd be ashamed to have a working wife. Feart of their whispers I suppose, them asking, can he not keep her then? Is he not a man?

I sat at the kitchen table this afternoon and built myself a parade of words with matches. I keep my brain clickering this way. I made one for you: MILL. That made me realise I could make KILL too. Then came HIM and MEN, and TIME. You could almost make a whole conversation of stick-words.

TELL HIM. MAKE ME. WHY.

How my mind runs around with me. I discovered the longest word yet.

FANKLE, I spelt. And I wondered if that's what we've got ourselves into, me and my husband, we've tangled ourselves in a great web of threads of what we each want and believe.

I stared a long time at the word FANKLE and then found I'd a wee tear to smudge out my eye before I left the house.

And they'll be glad to see me back too, those ones who walk past with a wee nod and soon after explode into sniggers and whispers.

He wants me to be happy, he says. So now, I'll remind him what's my intention.

One is for tweed
Two is for cotton
Three is for that letter not to be forgotten.

You. Sly witch.

Shrinking your walls around him, are you, aye, and all his jangling silly spindles and shuttles and lassies jumping and turning at his words? The poor wee man in there. Without a single lace-flimsy principle to pull around himself. Don't go thinking you can build a fortress around him. I'll scratch my fingernails on your harsh grey stone, pound open your door with these fists. Stand him at the top of that jaggy mountain if you want, I'd be marching right up there, my skirts all flicked up, snarling my bare feet on heather, to get at your Maister John Devlin.

He's lit my touch-paper right enough. Your doors and walls can't stop me. Even your Maister Knight, with his arms out like a gate across the door. And these railings, meant to close me out. They're nothing but a ring of black reeds that can be stamped flat. I'll get to him.

Tell me. Go on, tell me. How could he betray the Union? After all we fought for in Neilston. Didn't he support us then? And I have to get it from this newspaper – those lassies in there with their daft wee bent heads, forced to take on more machines and not a shilling extra to show for it. It was the Twisters who agreed to the deal, it says. Here, look. Read it if you can. And what choice did they have? What Union was representing them? 'All resolved peacefully,' it says. Like one happy family. Oh joy! I want some answers from your John Devlin in there.

It was a wee whispering party between you, right? Between you and Maister Knight and my husband in there, shrunk into a shadow by your shackles of grinding steel. You've got him spellbound with those crashing, clashing tunes you play on the looms.

Let him be warned. He'll be waving me off from the banks of the Clyde, on my way to the better life the paper promises every week. Then you'll get him all to yourself. Every last pinkie fingernail of him. He's got his hametoun life, got himself into the owner's pockets, got the box of matches into mine, the apron on, and me running for those stick-legged chickens of his. Is that all he wanted? When all the time I took him for a better man?

'Principles,' he says, 'aren't to brandish about in a wee family firm.'

You've stolen the John I knew.

Foul bitch. Eruption from the arse of the world. I'll leave you together. I'll wait for him in the house.

And wheesht. Harken to me you daft bitch. Harken to this wifie here who knows a thing or two.

Watch yourself.

So I've to lurk, is that it? I make myself one of your pals, the crows. It helps me wait. Aye, the crows make you bonny, a ring o daisies round your hat. Black daisies.

The second craw
fell and broke his jaw
fell and broke his jaw
fell and broke his jaw
on a cauld and frosty morning.

I've to spend my days waiting for an answer, rooting myself like some stubborn deep-rooted plant. Watching him from here in all his waking hours. Your haven for men and machines to make money together, with steel and wool and bolts and pulleys and power from water and steam.

He won't even look at me. He comes home after he's been with you, and hangs his silence on the back of the door. Like a great sagging overcoat, it drips till it fills the house right up to the ceilings. If he has any words for me at all, he says it's that he's tired from the night shifts. His days seem to run slow like the summer river.

When I asked for my train fare to Dundee, he hovered his hand over his purse, for all as if he might have stopped me going. And why? Because the memorial service was the same day as Maister Knight & Co.'s annual picnic. What does he think I've become? As if I would sit on that day under a Knight and Co. banner by some damned loch-side, sharing sandwiches with the greasy Carders and Spinners who've not even a penny's worth of intelligence between them. On *that* day.

What a crowd there was. That many men as well as women, all of us greetin, faces wet, and the Madonna lilies pure and beautiful and the purple and silver banners, and the words flying out brave, *Fight On and God Will Give the Victory.* What a flood went through me, of grief and gratitude, that she would die for us women, for the lassies of the future to be free, and able to work, and own their time, and say for themselves what will happen to them. I still feel the tears burning on my face now, and me and Annie clinging together, arms cleeked. And at least we know, for God-almighty sure. It will be hopeless to ignore us now.

John and I shared a sour-tasting silent meal at our kitchen table last night. What for? For I took the courage to stand up in the kirk and cry out, 'God Bless Emily Davison!' My hands were shaking and my voice sounded thin and high. But I did it. And John led me out by my wrist and wouldn't speak about it on the way home, walking off ahead with his head bent and bobbing. He didn't turn when I called out, stalking behind him. Maybe he's already going deaf, even at his age, the way all your weavers do. Right enough I have to shout at his back when he's sat at his desk with his head drooping forwards. He doesn't hear a thing. Or he makes it seem that way.

It's just one of the ways that you get your power over them, eh? Lay down your ear on the village street. What do you hear? Aye, that there's a war coming, of course.

This morning I went out to answer a chap on the door. No-one. A box on the doorstep lettered, 'Votes for Women'. As I bent to lift it, the box skidded away from me up the garden path, and I stamped out after it and there were boys in a tangle of string and mean laughter. They earned the boot in the ribs they took.

You're to blame. Buttressing up traditional ways, keeping women enslaved. And that's not it. You're making them hate me. I know you are. And you're forcing a hard bar of machined steel between me and John.

I sit alone at the kitchen table, building words. LAMENT is the one I found tonight. And then I couldn't settle because of the feeling in my chest, like a furnace, so I had to run away from it. To here. To you. For all the comfort you give me. For all it's your fault.

And do you know the worst thing, the very worst? It's what I read in his face. How he means to stop me from my own life. His look says it.

It says there's no question of signing that letter.

But I'll wait. He knows in his heart what is just, I'm sure of it.

I'll wait for him to change his mind. Do you not think I've learnt a thing or two from my sisters? The ones put in prison, who've refused food. They get taken to Perth and tied down and tubes of gruel are forced down their gullets till their stomachs heave like some creature has burrowed inside them. But they fight all the harder.

I can wait till the end of the world.

It's that dull to sit here and blether with you in the dark. Just like a wake, sitting up all night in the same room as the coffin. Keeping the dead company between the dying and the burying. But at most of the wakes I've been to, you get to play cards or drink tea, and something stronger if you haven't signed the pledge, aye, to keep you from sleep. What've I got to keep me awake? Just your old clankings and whirrings through walls and windows, steam gushing up above you in big puffs from the engine. You think that's enough to keep me going through the night? You wouldn't bother your ginger to put on a wee show for me, eh?

Ah well, ah well. Waiting and waiting. And how much longer is this night, this wake, till my ghost of a husband comes out as usual, and walks past me up the street, going home without looking at me or speaking?

Aye here I am. Still here. Your constant shadow. I've counted every one of your windows till I'm heart-roasted. The rhymes I've told to you. In and out. Round and round.

One, two, three a –leerie. Four, five, six a –leerie.

A hunner and ninety nine

My father fell in a byne.

And how is it you never join in? I just play by myself till my eyes are going thigether.

And I can't hold my head up, sitting here as if I'm a fire that's been left to glow in the hearth at night. My poor wee head drops and that's when the dreams crowd in on me. There's the ship, and the coffin with its white lilies, and the field of banners rippling through the Trongate on the way to Glasgow Green. All the pictures dunting me. And then John's leaning down and kissing me and he's got his rough edges back, grazing my cheek, so I can feel it here, right here, even through the dream. I dream of his hand with a pen in it, signing my letter, and we both do a wee dance around the room, throwing things in the air like we're jugglers from the circus.

But I wake. The footsteps clanking past. I lift my head, my glued-down eyes, to see the men coming from the pub with barbed spines on their backs as they turn from looking at me. And I feel the slither of spittle on my chin, where it fell when I was sleeping. John's crushed away from me behind your glass and rock, and your smell's teasing my nostrils awake, a sickly, howling smell.

I make pictures in my mind too, to pass the time. You're forcing them cruel. Try this one. John, standing there in your doorway, and there's a band of women marchers looking for what's theirs, pushing towards him, till he's pressed against you, hands feeling back for you, clinging. He's just like Maister Hough, that feartie manager at Neilston. Aye, and then they're lifting him up on their shoulders, all limp and powerless, and heading for a great pile of timber in the field, to fling him atop of, and there's a can of paraffin waiting. All that's needed is the spark.

And I'd have to tell him, 'This was coming, you saw it coming, eh? But would you listen to a woman? Would you listen to your wife? Would you hell.'

How all that loving can turn to a hot stake skewered in the gut.

And so I'll sit here. On and on.

I can wait harder. Oh aye.

It still glides in to the dock. The ship. My dreams shiver in that minute of shut-eye between staring at you and my head falling. I hear the slipping it makes in the water as it leaves, and the cries and cheers of the crowds as they go. And it vanishes to a wee sparkle in the waves as it catches the light. It vanishes right away.

And I think how that would look to John if he was standing on the dock to wave me off. And I wonder if he'd be able to see from that distance how I take off the apron, and pull out the box of matches from my pocket, and open it up and scatter the matches into the wind. They settle into the water, and all the fires I might have made in the stove for him soften into mush and sink away. How a tear might slide down his face for the old times – the marching side by side, the dancing, the times in bed.

Oh aye. I can greet too. I still have tender parts. So I do. So, so, so. And only my own arms to crawl into.

And why do I sit like an idiot and blether to you? You bitch. It's you I should hate. You took him from me. You sit there fat and smug and stealing from us all. Stealing the goodness from our men, and the money from our purses to make yourself Maister Knight's fat pup-dog. How you suck us dry.

See how I've learnt to spit like a man. Take that. The worst festers from my lungs – yellow and poisonous. It's all for you.

Here's men passing. 'And what is it you're looking at? You'll get the same cure as that bitch, so you will. Aye, what bitch? What bitch? Deleerit, deleerit, so I am.'

Gone to their beds. Gone home to their poor wives. Voices fading.

My own arms tight. Crawling home. So so so.

Feel me here, can you? Sneaking behind you. If my husband

looks out now, he'll see a torn-faced wretch across the river. Aye, here I am, hung in the bristling bare branches, gnawing at them, as if they're the bars of my cage. Papery bark gumming my mouth, tasting of salt and stagnant rain, and men's sex. But he'll not look out. He's bolted up inside you. Sold himself to you. Like all of them in there, not a free soul amongst them.

You hardly know I'm here do you, with your back windows dusty and green with damp. It's a clapped-in face you have from this side, not the pretty silver glister you like to flaunt to the street, and your oh-so-sparkling clear eyes. You're a sham. Mossy, with the damp risen from the river. Clammy and gangrenous. Those buildings for the dyeing and warping and finishing crawl around you, low and grovelling. It's a rare midden you are.

Do you feel me here?

I've to hide from the street, from the village folk giving me black sinkers as they pass, and the weans calling me a loop. And I might be going round greetin, with my mouth pulled open, my hair in tails and ash smearing my face, calling names at you, and throwing curses at him pressed as he is behind your glass. But whose fault would that be?

Whose?

Answer, will you?

Am I no loud enough for you? Is it the rattling of the branches that's clogged your lugs?

Breathe, breathe, breathe. One two three. How it hurts in my chest. Like I've been skewered on a hot sword. It hurts and hurts. Why do I shake so?

Here's matches still rattling in my pocket. A habit now. I found another word. It's spelt out on the kitchen table for him to read for himself when he comes home to the cold kitchen and he can't avoid me anymore. The R's are strange and the O is square, but he'll understand well enough.

TRAITOR.

He wants me in the home to toil over the stove, and the laundry, and hardening my hands in the soil. And in the bed I suppose. He's one of the men say they support us until their next meal doesn't arrive. They conspire with the cooking pot. They believe in freedom for people, oh aye, as long as the people are men. And you're a machine for the lining of men's pockets, for men to wear tweeds for killing, and uniforms of war. You're the one's made him how he is.

And now it's all over. I've cleaned the hearth each morning, like a proper wee wife. And this morning, I found it. A scrap of paper left amongst the ashes. A wee triangle from the corner of a larger sheet. The long edge singed brown by the flames. Good quality paper, cream coloured, stiff. I knew the crest in red and gold – had stroked my finger over it that many times. Just a wee bit of it was left.

And in the corner a greasy thumb had printed onto it a badge to say who it was had thrown my hopes and freedom into the fire. My hands fell deep into the soft ashes, but they were cold, all cold. My face in ashes, breathing them in, clogging my nostrils.

Only in my heart the flames beat on.

2006

Broken Symmetry

Tom was walking in the dark and there was a white shape ahead, blurry and undefined. It rose up, flapping. Then seemed to part into two.

He woke when Kirsten sat on the edge of the bed, opening his eyes to see her smile crumple.

'Hello,' she said. 'Not feeling so good now?'

Soft wings were still batting at him. He fought his way up and out of sleep. 'Just dozing,' he said.

'I saw you at the window, didn't I?'

He shrugged. 'How was your day?'

'Fine. I'll put the kettle on,' she said, and he felt the edge of the bed spring back up.

He heard her moving around, pulling blinds down to close the eyes of the place. She came back in with two mugs of tea and he sat up, shaking off the clutch of his dream. He'd been lying in bed most of the day with the radio playing – he hadn't been at the window as she seemed to think.

'What a difference since the clocks went back,' she said. 'It was like seeing the Mill when it was working. Could almost hear all the old machines whirring away.'

'How?'

'With lights on in so many windows. Rows of them.'

He didn't bother arguing but he knew she was wrong, unless there was an electrical fault, god forbid. Most of the other residents had jobs that kept them in Edinburgh during the week. They played at rural life in Perthshire only two days in seven, and wouldn't be back till tomorrow to start the weekend.

Kirsten soon stood up. 'I've some marking to do.'

And she went off, even though it was five o'clock and she'd had all that time at school after the children went home.

When they'd moved in a month before – with his conversion of the woollen mill to flats finally complete – he knew he'd have to rest up a bit. He'd lost weight. His ribs seemed to have risen to the surface of his body. The doctor had called it post-viral fatigue, said he'd have to give in to it, avoid any stress. But the new owners of the flats had other ideas. Living on site, even if he had designed for Kirsten and himself a unique home, hadn't been such a great idea. There were knocks on the door at least twice a day about the latest cupboard handle to fall off or loose skirting board.

He'd stopped answering the phone, disconnected the entry-phone, turned off his mobile. Instead, each evening Kirsten scribbled down answer-phone messages in a list which stayed on the kitchen counter, accumulating length. Each day he piled the post on top of it. Each evening, she brought the list back to the surface.

Kirsten came back into the bedroom with a torn envelope and a letter. She held it out to him.

'No spectacles,' he said, staying put.

'It's the Dawsons.'

He ran a hand through his hair. 'Number three?'

'Bath taps.'

He closed his eyes, and soon afterwards felt her weight settling near him, the bed tipping towards her.

'We have to get on top of this,' she said quietly.

She meant *him*. 'Yes,' he said. 'Yes.'

He'd first seen the four-storey Mill building several years before on the way to visit Kirsten's parents. The door was shackled with a huge chain and padlock and hung with a 'DANGER NO ENTRY' sign. There were gaping black holes in the roof through which crows dived and sprang out. The windows were glassless and black. Buddleia straggled out of gutters.

Tom had climbed through a ground floor window into a long hall where rows of black machines crowded, blocking out the light. The place had an almost sweet smell, and his fingers lifted from any surface with a sheen of grease, sticky with fluff. An impromptu skateboard park had been set up in there with ramps and jumps. Charred circles pock-marked the floor where fires had been lit, beer cans scattered nearby.

Despite its dereliction, he found something statuesque in the building. It dwarfed everything else in the village. Like a ruined abbey, it was not only fine in itself, but seemed to embody a noble past. He saw its potential, having worked on large-scale industrial buildings before: the conversion of a church into a climbing centre in Edinburgh, a warehouse into flats. He specified only the best, authentic materials, getting exasperated with clients who wanted to compromise on quality. Perhaps, at the age of only thirty-four, the Mill could be his *pièce de résistance*.

He'd read his business plan to Kirsten: 'The host building will be stripped back to expose its essential qualities and original features contrasted with carefully selected contemporary materials making it fit for a new function.'

She frowned. 'Isn't it really a home we need?'

'Ah, but it will be.'

He reckoned they could sell seven flats, having bought the building for a song, and keep for themselves the top left corner. In their flat he'd minimise the boxing-in of the space to maintain an industrial feel, a large gallery-style room, and make best use of light converging from two facing walls of windows. It would be divided by the marching line of cast-iron pillars that gave the building its skeleton.

'Why's it lopsided?' she'd said once when they were standing on the street staring up at the Mill's dark face.

'What do you mean?'

'It looks like something's missing.' She pointed at the single bell tower on the west end. 'Shouldn't there be one each end?'

She was right of course but he wasn't concentrating on that; was already visualising the article in *The Architects' Journal*, the photo of them in the long, light gallery. His arm would be around Kirsten's shoulder. Her black hair and a smile, rather than a frown, would be glossed up by sunlight.

Friday morning, the sun was throwing bright trapezoids, criss-crossed by window bars, onto the oak floorboards. He stood with a mug of tea in his hand, looking south. The mountain was there, its triangle of high rock taunting him.

Moving to the other side, he looked north into the car park and the street below where a bench faced the building. Someone sitting there before the Mill was built in 1831 would have had a view directly to the hills. But now, it offered only a cold place to sit in the Mill's shadow.

As he backed away from the window, an oil stain ghosting through the paint on the wall above it made him pause. A fault he'd been trying to ignore. He went to look for the stain-blocking paint; reckoned on having two good hours in which to do something constructive that would impress Kirsten when she got in from work.

One of the old weavers, George Kaye, had come in once when work was underway, a big lurching Yorkshireman who leant towards Tom when he spoke, puffing cigarette-halitosis over him. He still lived in the village and had wanted to see what they were up to. He was deaf as a post. Despite his age, he led Tom at a furious arthritic-hip hobble through the building, telling him how everything used to be. He shook his head at the plasterboard going up, boxing in new, neat rooms, hiding the great bare boulders of rock that made the walls.

'Should have knocked it down. Started again. You have no idea.'

'Oh?' Tom bristled.

'No idea.' George shook his head at the lengths of architrave on the floor that would case the windows, the wiring writhing from a hole near the door where the entry-phone would be. 'No idea what's gone on in this place.'

Tom heard an accusation. 'It's a sound, strong building,' he'd said slowly. 'It'd be criminal not to use it for something.'

When George's tour reached the part of the building where their own flat was to be, right below Kirsten's missing bell tower, the weaver gave little shifty glances around, taking in the original features Tom had chosen to preserve. He pointed to the place where the yellow stain now rose through new paint.

'You'll never cover that up,' he'd bellowed. 'It's where the main drive shaft came in. Drenched the place in oil for two or three lifetimes.' He explained that it had coupled to the spinning frame on this floor, something called a 'Mule', a machine that wound yarn by moving forwards and backwards in long sweeps. A lad would have gone to and fro with it, he said, watching for broken threads, walking twenty miles a day.

'Aye, it was work went on here, lad. Graft. You could never call it a home.'

'Well, we intend to,' Tom said.

Kirsten, who had come in, was hovering close by, listening.

George greeted her as he turned on his heel and lurched back down the stairs. Through a window Tom watched him pass the salvage skips lined up in the car park. Bobbins and cones wrapped with coloured yarn made mountains in one skip. Ranks of erect spindles sparred up in a confused heap in another. George reached out to touch the cast-iron casing of a spinning frame that was waiting for the scrap-dealer. 'HATTERSLEY, 1914', it proclaimed, approaching its centenary in two pieces, shattered by a jagged crack.

Kirsten came up behind him at the window. 'Do you think he's got a point?'

He span around to face her. 'About what?'

'It wasn't built for this.'

'So what?' He was getting tired of her lack of support.

She hesitated. 'Bad vibes?'

'Hippy,' he'd said.

She looked around when she came in on Friday evening, then

fixed on where the stain had been, and smiled. 'You've been busy,' she said, and leant to kiss the top of his head.

He felt like one of her ten-year-old pupils but tried to brush aside the irritation. After all, it was exactly the reward he'd been seeking.

'That's good,' she said. 'That you felt up to doing it.'

He saw her gaze move onto the counter, to the snagging list. She went and stood over it, as if that was them 'getting on top of it'.

In the night he lay blinking in the moments after waking with the sense that a noise had disturbed him. A great sigh as the building exhaled perhaps, heaving with its weekend cargo of sleepers.

The noise came again. Some sort of cry or screech. A suggestion of something knocking against glass. He'd known crows to settle on window ledges at first light and peck at their own reflections. But it was still too early for that.

He could just make out the dark half-moons curving under Kirsten's eyes. Wide awake now, he got up, closing the door of the bedroom behind him. The knock came again, right in front of him at one of the windows which faced the street.

He'd wanted to use a special glass that transformed from transparent to opaque at the flick of a switch. It was an ingenious sandwich – liquid crystals between two panes. He'd read that they were having some fun with it in Prada changing rooms in New York but would have been the first to use it in this kind of building. Turned out it wasn't feasible with sash windows and even what he *had* done was too expensive. Everything was too expensive. He hadn't quite dared to look at his bank statements recently.

Releasing the blind, he faced the dark, portioned into squares by the window bars. There was no apparition; no faces, no hands. Just the dark. His eyes began to adjust: the car park dim below, and the path which led between the heavy main door of the building and the wrought-iron gate.

A shadow across the gate now detached itself and moved swiftly away along the street, merging with the gloom. Perhaps there were foxes out there, he thought, rifling the bins. But just himself as a representative of human life.

They got up late on Saturday morning and Kirsten went to the village Spar for fake French pastries. It was her way of retrieving a bit of their Edinburgh life.

He made coffee while she was out and opened each blind in turn, finishing at the one he'd stood at in the night.

Kirsten came in and kissed him, face polished pink by cold. 'It's a gorgeous day. Do you feel up to a walk?'

Her question sunk him onto one of the kitchen stools. 'Let's see,' he said. 'After coffee. I'll see how I feel, hey?'

He knew to avoid tarnishing her brightness. But he hadn't left the building, or even the flat, for two weeks now, confined by the thought of the long clattering descent through six flights of stairs. He'd be humiliated by the stops to rest on the climb back up, and risk running into whingeing residents.

The sunlight burst into the room from the direction of the hill to the south, firing up red highlights in Kirsten's hair, and making her squint.

She moved to stand at the north window with her coffee and he lay back on the sofa. Any comfort fractured when he noticed that in this particular light, a shadowy yellow stain was already seeping through fresh paint, pointing down towards the window above Kirsten's head.

He noticed again the dark half-moons under her eyes. They'd both had the idea that rural life would be calmer and slower. Her new job seemed harder than ever.

'I heard a noise last night,' he said.

'What?'

'Don't know,' he said. 'Something flying into that window maybe.'

'What, like an owl?'

'Maybe. I couldn't see it.' The idea for some reason rebalanced him. 'We'll have to get an anti-owl device.'

'They used to nail owls across doors to keep storms away, you know,' she said.

'Really?'

'According to Grandad. Protecting barns from damage. Been doing a topic on owls with my class. Did you know some say they take souls of the dead to the afterlife too?'

He tried to join in. 'And wise, eh?'

'There's an old nursery rhyme,' she said.

'*There was an owl lived in an oak*
The more he heard, the less he spoke.
The less he spoke, the more he heard.
O, if men were all like that wise bird.'

Was she getting at him? 'You've done your homework,' he said.

There were a few moments of silence. She went to the dreaded list and he felt a gathering.

'We could at least make a start.'

It began again, a discussion of where the priorities lay.

'Can't it wait till I get better?'

'You may not be up to full strength for a while.'

'Come off it!'

'Well, you know these post-viral things…' And after a moment she added. 'Isn't there someone you could pay on a daily rate?'

He thought for a moment or two but there was only one logical answer. 'There's Sally.'

'Sally?' Kirsten looked up swiftly. 'She's probably out of the country.'

'I'll find out,' he said.

He went back to bed, curling into a tight ball and waited for her to return from her walk.

'If you could deal with this lot, I'll probably start feeling better.' He dangled before Sally the ever-growing list of snags.

'Funny how none of the problems are in your own flat, bro,' she said. 'Higher standards, eh?'

'Well, you could sort that out.' He pointed up to the stain.

'Oil,' she said, and then moved closer so she was underneath it, looking up. 'Is that a crack?'

He shrugged. 'Plasterwork settling.'

She gave him one of her sceptical looks.

His sister Sally had been his 'right-hand woman' for the early stages of the conversion. She'd done the engineering calculations and was able at general building jobs. They used to climb together as teenagers, going higher, steeper, harder, to avoid their parents' rows at home. They had trust.

She was always off travelling and when in Britain lived in a camper-van that she pulled off a road until someone objected. He thought of her as a migratory bird, her body stringy from the miles covered, bringing ticks and other parasites hidden in her feathers from the southern hemisphere.

He liked the idea of having both Kirsten and Sally around

him; one on each side, offering different strengths. But he knew Kirsten found Sally difficult.

With the camper-van in the Mill car park, Sally worked up through the building in her size eight steel-toe-capped boots with a ladder over one shoulder, and a nail belt around her waist. He wondered what the residents would make of her – tall, a nose stud, short blonde hair and a roll-up behind one ear. She wasn't much like the local builders.

When he was drifting towards sleep, he sometimes heard strange rhythms – whirring, banging – coming from below, distorting into syllables like speech or song. Sally, drilling or sanding, he supposed; the building restless beneath him. He felt pushed ever higher into its top eastern corner where the second bell tower used to be.

Sally was sitting with him one afternoon as the sky dimmed and rectangles of black glass surrounded them. He hushed her as she started to say something.

He was aware of his own pulse knocking in his temple, like a rotating piece of machinery. 'Can you hear anything?' he asked.

'Just the drone of boredom,' she said. 'You're quite dull these days you know.'

'You're right. I *can* hear something,' Sally said, one afternoon soon after. She came in, dropping her nail belt near the door and walking dusty bootprints towards the kettle.

Tom listened. A ferocious gale was roaring down the valley to wallop against the Mill's western gable.

'The wind,' he said.

'No.' Sally stood still, an ear raised towards the ceiling. 'I mean that groaning from the roof.'

He heard it then. The ship-creak of timbers.

When he glanced upwards, he saw that the crack in the plaster had got longer. He asked Sally to have a look in the loft, and she returned, shedding cobwebs, summer-crisped bluebottles, dark feathers from her hair and boiler suit. She was frowning.

'Didn't we talk about putting in some tie rods?' she said.

'We talked about it but decided it wasn't necessary.' He'd heard an edge of accusation in her voice, and added, 'according to your calculations.'

'We?' she queried. 'You must have made that decision after I left. I was going off to New Zealand, remember?'

Above them the roof made its point, a great sigh shuddering as a new gust caught the gable. There was a series of small after-shocks.

'Something's going on up there,' she said. 'It seems unstable.'

'Don't be daft.'

She was over-reacting. This great hulking building was as solid as the mountain that it faced to the south.

'Cup of tea?' he said, hoping that she would make it.

'Tom! Look at that.'

He followed her gaze to where the plaster had crazed into a web of fine lines on the ceiling between the pillars.

'Did you keep my calculations?' she asked.

'Filed,' he said. 'Somewhere.' He gestured at the door to the spare room where boxes and papers had been piled up and abandoned when they moved in.

'You know there are some old repairs up there in the roof?' she said.

He shrugged. 'It's an old building. We checked it was structurally sound.'

'And it was.'

'Exactly,' he said. 'So what are you worrying about it for? All timber moves, doesn't it. It accommodates. That's the beauty of it.'

'So, has Sally nearly finished?' Kirsten asked one morning.

'More or less,' he said.

The day before, Sally's work had reached their corner of the building. He'd asked her to plaster over the cracks, and then paint.

She'd protested: 'Is it really worth it when the whole building might fall down?'

He'd told her not to exaggerate.

'So that's it then?' said Kirsten. 'We're done?'

'Probably.'

'Probably?'

'She's having a look at the roof too.'

'The roof? Why?'

'Probably nothing. But you heard the creaks and groans last week. We just want to be sure.'

'Of what?'

'Its solidity.'

She was leaving for work. She had a bag in her hand, her hat already on her head. She stared at him. 'Isn't that a bit fundamental?'

'Like I said, we're just being sure.'

Her arms dropped to her sides.

He looked at his watch. 'Hadn't you better get going?'

Later he put a cake in the oven, and then went to lie down. Not long afterwards Sally barged in.

'Fuck's sake,' she said. 'What are you burning?'

'Shit,' he said, 'the cake.' And went to rescue it, the oven door pouring smoke into the room. 'Open a window, would you?'

'I was looking at the roof from down there,' she said, pointing to the bench on the street. 'What slates did you use?'

'Delabole, of course,' he said. 'The Rolls-Royce of slate.'

She swivelled round and spat out: 'Idiot.'

'Quality, sis.'

She circled back so she could look him in the eye, then said slowly, 'And the heaviest.'

'So?'

'We specified standard. And I distinctly remember recommending an extra inspection to make sure the roof was in perfect condition or if not, to shove a tie-rod in, to be on the safe side.'

Tom was squinting through smoke, grappling for memory. 'It was a long time ago.'

'So perhaps you've also forgotten that you accused me of over-specifying,' she said.

'Did I?'

'Called me a "girly", if I remember rightly.'

He snorted.

'All that extra weight could collapse the tiniest weakness in the trusses.' Sally glared at him.

'Why would there be any weakness? That's ridiculous.' Tom lay back on the sofa and held a cushion to his face.

A fresh gust came out of a relatively still day. The roof above them sighed; a deep, painful creak. They both looked up.

When Kirsten came in from work, the cold seemed to stream off her. He'd left the plans lying open on the floor. The edges lifted when she moved.

'What's with the plans?'

'Trusses.' He waved a hand vaguely at them.

'Trusses?'

Nodding made him feel sick.

She sat down next to him. 'You'll have to tell me more.'

He pointed a finger towards the ceiling. 'In the roof. The original trusses might have been dodgy.'

'Why would they be dodgy?'

'Who knows? Perhaps earlier damage we didn't know about.'

'Damage from what?'

He shrugged. 'Subsidence. Poor workmanship. Some trauma or other. Who knows?'

A silence hung for a moment. He saw her look at the yellow bruise high on the wall, the crack still exposed where Sally, in the end, had refused to cover it. Kirsten was biting her lip. He thought for a moment she might cry. He gathered up energy from some remote depths and reached for her hand.

'Don't worry,' he said. 'We'll sort it out.'

She looked at him, still frowning. 'You mean, you and Sally?'

He nodded, although he had no idea where Sally was and whether her huff would allow her to come back.

Kirsten's frown didn't lift. 'I was just about to buy a Christmas tree, start putting up some decorations.'

He didn't move, didn't breathe, didn't look at her.

'Don't be daft,' he said finally, and then, more certainly: 'We won't have to move out. Nothing like that. Get a tree.'

It was as if in the precise moment he woke in the night, the room had transformed back to silence.

Kirsten woke too, reached out and touched his shoulder. 'What is it? Why are you so sweaty?'

'Did you hear anything?'

'Mmm?' She pulled him down, cradled his shivering body. 'Come back to sleep.'

'Stay awake with me. Just for ten minutes. Then I'll be okay.'

But sleep soon swam her away from him.

He got up. The floor chilled the soles of his feet, the building transformed by night, stretching upwards, leaving him on a high, remote point, exposed to swaying, precarious air. But he would not climb down.

Nor would he turn on his phone and text Sally to find out where she was.

He saw Sally at dusk the next day, slouched on the bench, long legs pushed out in front, and kicked into crossed ankles. She seemed to be regarding the thirty-six glass 'eyes' of the building and, no doubt, the roof.

Then he saw another figure lurching towards her along the street. George Kaye. He stopped next to the bench, propped on a stick and seemed to be listening to her, leaning in as if he might topple. Then he straightened, jabbed his stick in the direction of the building. She seemed to offer him something out of her pocket, perhaps her phone. But he turned with apparent determination and hobbled away, back in the direction he'd come from.

Tom dropped the blinds; shut Sally out. Kirsten was out late at the school parents' night. He dozed on the sofa, put on the TV for company. A gale warning was issued on the news at six o'clock.

Some time later, through layers of fog he heard a buzz. Followed by another. Buzzes further away, in different parts of the building. Doors opening, clicking closed. Footsteps descending; voices echoing. Workers leaving at the end of the day, tripping down to the big door and out the gate. But he was not a worker here; he was in charge. He remained.

He caught again at the tail of a dream.

Sometime later he woke, went to a window. The corner of the blind sprang up out of his hands, baring the glass. And below, he saw a man with a hard hat and a clipboard surrounded by a small crowd of people – residents from number five, from number seven. The man looked up and his hand rose in a beckoning motion.

And now Sally was with the man. They both looked up at the window, and Sally's arm cranked up in an angry summons. When he didn't respond, Sally led the man to the main door, presumably to let him in using her key. Tom heard footsteps climbing steadily towards him, and finally the man's uneven breathing. There was a sharp knock.

The man held up a Perth and Kinross Council card when Tom opened the door.

'Building Control,' he said. 'We've a report of a safety issue. We're obliged to evacuate while we make an inspection.'

'I didn't report anything.'

'No sir. Someone else did. Now if you wouldn't mind?' He gestured at Tom to go with him towards the stairs. 'You're the last. I believe you were the architect of the conversion?'

'Isn't this a bit of an overreaction?'

'Gales forecast tonight, sir. We heard it's the roof in question.'

Sally. She must have phoned them.

Everything seemed to list so that Tom was being swept with plates and upturned tables and people's discarded jackets across the inner decks of a storm-bound ship. Washed first towards one end and then the other, he clung to stable things – the base of a cast iron pillar; his fingernails gouging into the timber of the floor.

He felt his arm grabbed above the elbow. The floor levelled again. The inspector puffed himself up, pursed his lips. 'Sir. I need you to leave now.'

The door clicked shut behind them; lights left blazing, and they were into the echoing stairwell. A sharp crack ricocheted from above and as he took the first steps down, the sound materialised into something he could visualise – an apex heaving itself out of alignment.

When they reached a landing he paused, looked out of the window, saw Kirsten, Sally, George Kaye, all huddled together.

The inspector propelled him on again.

Two flights to the next landing. He looked again from this window. Faces were starting to be revealed rather than the tops of heads.

The rhythm of the descent was established, the white walls echoing their footsteps. They reached the final landing and paused. Being only one flight above the ground, he had a new perspective. He saw Kirsten's pale face, her shoulders rounded as if braced against something.

The inspector nudged Tom on. The door at the bottom opened with a rush of cold, black air, numbing his nostrils, suffocating him for a moment.

Expectant faces. A clamour of voices. The wind inflated his shirt, scouring around his ribs. And then he was on the street, sitting on the bench.

'Hear that?' Sally's arms were folded. She nodded towards the building as the wind battered audible creaks from the roof.

He distantly heard George say to Sally, 'Lad wouldn't listen, eh?' Then George sank his old crooked body heavily onto the bench beside Tom. The pair of them looked up at the Mill. A few windows glimmered with light still, one decorated with paper snowflakes. But it was somehow obvious that the building had been abandoned once again.

He breathed in and as he let it go, something hefty like a sob seemed to escape from the top of his ribcage. At the same moment, a white shape took moth-like flight from somewhere above the Mill's door, almost as if it had squeezed out of a crack between two blocks of stone. A silvery light glanced briefly from its beating form before it was swallowed by the night.

'Owl,' Kirsten said from somewhere behind him.

George raised a hand as if he might pat Tom's leg, but then let it fall again to his own. 'Aye, it's empty now,' he said. Not long afterwards he got up and hobbled away.

Sally slumped down in George's place on the bench. And then, on Tom's other side, a cool hand landed on his forearm.

'You should have brought a jacket down,' Kirsten said.

'You're right,' he said.

He heard a slight snort from Sally.

'You're right,' he repeated, and took a deep, clean breath in and out.

July 1914

Strike

So you've pulled a hush down about you, now the strikers are away home and the night shift abandoned? Your face through the railings is as crabby as always. A last glint of the gloaming dying in all your windows. You're a joke, eh – a mill that's dark, like an out-of-season theatre. These crows are ready to start pecking at you, as if you're a rotten corpse. Ha! Didn't I tell you this time would come?

There's a shiver creaking up and down my skirts, and the wind's whipping around my ankles. I'll no stay for long. The night's about to be lit up with moon, and my scalp's shrinking to a doll's.

I've come just to girn and gripe at you one last time. Aye, don't bother thinking you can beat me at ugly looks. And you'll know of course, it's not just your hackit self I've come to see. I've to talk to him that's still inside. Aye, I see his lamplight glowing up there. The feartie's not dared come home yet. I've to tell him how I'm away tomorrow, and where I'm going. I can't say I'm looking forward to the sea-sickness, but I'm minding the better life that's waiting for me at the other side.

I got my farewell gift the day, did I not? At last, those

glaikit mill-lassies turned their heads upwards and opened their mouths into snarls. And didn't I laugh to see you pulling yourself to your full four floors' of height, a bell tower at each end pointing up like a brave pair of ears. But there's not a peck of the tyrant in you now. It's all bluff.

A crowd of lassies you had around you, eh, chanting, and hurling their fists, rubbing up sparks between themselves. Even the ones who wouldn't join the Union were barracked out to swarm around your gates in a wicked smoke-haze. They're in the same mind as workers in every mill in the country. All out in sympathy. And that's a bigger power of good than the one you think you do in there – making cloth, manufacturing money.

They're bees in a hive, the mill-girls. They buzz with industry, strive and toil to make a honeycomb, and then along comes the enterprising man, the bee-keeper, who lifts it and what does he do with it? Aye, he takes it all for himself. He doesn't give them even a tottie wee drop of it. But they've got wise to him now. They're buzzing. And they'll jag Maister Knight with their dark, sticky stings. And his freakish shadows, the foremen, who lurk in the corners, not sure where they belong – out or in.

It wasn't your ranks of windows I was forced to count today, like I usually do to make time go past. It was heads I counted, heads that bobbed and bounced and turned to each other. More heads than windows. *One, two, three, aleerie.* I couldn't count them all, I'd not enough fingers. The place was loupin and I was amongst them, without anyone flinching from me, pointing fingers at the crabbit wifie. I was just another lassie the day.

Haven't the Pankhursts always told us 'deeds not words'? And finally it's happening here in this bug-bitten village of numpties with their 'yes-Maister-Knight' ways. Didn't I always say it was possible?

And look at me. I've become strong in place of you. See how flint I am with these matches in my apron pocket. Aye, and I'm still proud of that thing I helped do with them. I haven't even cheeped of it – I mustn't. But I watched it march in giant letters across the front page of every newspaper in the land.

Wheesht, don't make me say. I'm keeping it in here, hidlins.

So I've a plan. I've savings, from my days at the big house and from the dismal work I've done howkin tatties in the mud with the tinkers, my scarf pulled up so they couldn't see whose wife I was. I've been collecting things into a box under the bed, the things I'll need over there in Canada. Stockings and linen and cutlery – there's even amongst it some silver spoons I've been shining up. He won't give me my freedom here, doesn't want to give his wife her right to work. So I shall take it, what's rightfully mine, in another land.

I saw that shadow of him the day. Aye, he was hanging back behind the window, just a smudge of him leaking around the casement, so he could see the stooshie going on out here. He's all in a fankle because of the deal he's made for weaving the khakis. And this strike-bother's got right in the road of delivering on time.

So you're no sleeping yet, is that it, on account of him? I can see the wee gomeril, up on the top floor. His head's like a picture in the window, bowed over the spinning frame, mending threads. There's a glow of lamp around him and a distant hum. Working alone. The only one, while the sympathy strike goes on. Keeping the place going like the loyal foreman that he's become, as two-faced as the Briggait clock.

I mind him at those Union meetings in Glasgow, fierce for workers' rights. You couldn't help watching for the heart of the man that shone out his face. Wouldn't he have been the loudest voice, up on a box with his fist pumping? Now look at him. Complouterin with your Maister Knight. Aye but my frenzy's behind me. If that's what he wants. You take him! Have him. You're welcome, each to the other.

Now. I've just to tell him goodbye. I've to tell him myself, of course. He's still my husband, mind. You'll let me in for old times? Just once, into the places you've kept secret from me all this time. Mind how we were pals, how we listened to each other's patter once? You'll be free of me tomorrow. So you'll let me in, eh?

Through your gate. My hand grazing on the rough cast of your wall. You've still the faded patch on your door where they scraped away my poster. You remember our wee joke? You looked so bonnie for that blink in time, decorated green and purple. Just for a flash it was there before they peeled it off, before John's anger came like a swipe from a dozing cat.

'You want to make a fool of me to Maister Knight, now I'm foreman?' he said.

I flared at him, 'So it's an angel you want is it – not a woman that acts for her beliefs?'

But later we made it up, in the usual way. That sweet fire we share. We shared. Oh so we did. So so we did.

Hush, gowk. It's no the time for greetin.

Ear to the door. The looms silent-dead tonight, but a faint whirr of the spinning on your top floor. He's keeping Knight & Company going on his own. Who needs a whole army of workers when you've Maister John Devlin?

Now, latch. Open up.

Locked?

Locked himself in. Damned feartie. Locked? Take my fists.

Let.

Me.

In.

Right you are, witch. Stand in my road and I'll make him hear another way, above your clatterings and gnashings.

Aye, this is the one. This rock. Hard and coarse, grating in my hand. You display your workers in there like wee pinned moths in a glass-topped box, eh? You grind souls into money for Maister Knight. But look at these shoulders. They're coiled with hard strength, so they are. Don't you doubt it. I'll break that glass face of yours.

There it goes. Upwards, fast and hard. Hark to the shriek that comes out of me. It feels like freedom. Take that for all the lassies to come, for the freedom of them all.

Spangles shattering and clattering through the air fall back on me. Arms around my head. And now, look at the dark scar that's made your first floor squint-faced. You've a black unblinking eye now for the crows to pass through.

Heartbeats. Breath. The wind beating at me. Nothing else. Nothing, damn him. No answer. What could follow it in then, to catch his eye?

It needs a colour, something to spark attention. A flame. That's it. The rattle's still there in my pocket. The rattle he yoked me to, showing me my job. Kitchen matches. Not to cook his dinner the night. Not to arrange in words on the table. It's deeds that matter now, mind?

Strike.

Flaring into my face.

Onto what? Here, the silver-shining cloth, still soaked in spirit, wrapping another rock. Flames, ouch, nipping at my fingers. Up again, through the gash. Up. An arc of orange flame against the night.

And the whole world this time, will have heard my screech,

that flew up to the top of that pointed crag above you, and down into the dark roots of the earth, eh? And all today's lassies cheering me on, if they could see.

Now will you let me in?

Back from you, back to the gate, to look up. I see his head through the top floor window, still bent at the frame, moving along it like the good attendant. He sees nothing outside, hears nothing yet.

There! On the first floor, something's starting. Mist rising, and then red amongst the looms. A glow, just like at Strathearn. 'Wait until you see it catch, then away, fast.' That was the instructions for the action on the Perthshire mansions.

The first lick of flame against glass. The clash and clatter of it bursting out. He must hear now. He must smell the black air rising up towards him through wood and grease. Oh my heart. Drumming so's my lugs are plugged with it.

He'll need to come out now. He's to speak with his wife. He'll need to get out here. Fast.

A flash and clatter follow me out through the gate onto the street. Another window exploding. Turning back. There he is, framed in the window, looking to see what's happening. Your drive shafts turn hell's wheels behind him. One hand's up, his arm crooked over his head, his face dark against the light behind. A skitter of bats in me, flapping, rising to fill my throat.

John!

Get out now.

The flames light up the yard and dance like a sea between us. Heat pushes me back a step, into the shadow. And another step. My hand flutters up into a wave. I hold it in the night air a wee minute but I don't know if he sees my goodbye through your pandemonium of thrashing flame. My hand falls back to my side, and I burrow it into my coat pocket as I turn away down the dark road.

I win one last glance back and see how the red seethes in your windows, rises beneath him. Then I start to run.

2019

The Other Side of Stone

Jade stumbled out of the minibus, blinking. They'd only come thirty miles or so from Perth but it was fucking endless. Tiny roads following lochs and prickly forests, then a river. Mountains on either side, dark and light, patchy like an army camouflage jacket.

Dog-drowsy now, she sat on a low wall in the car park, smoking alongside a couple of others. Three streets struck off from here, grey stone cottages shrinking like cowards under a rock wall that reared up behind the village.

She was here for the apples. She'd been lectured over the last months about picking, storing, pickling them, and now she was finally out in 'the field', as they called it.

Alarm had jangled in her mum's eyes as she said: 'You'll not be back at lunchtime, then?'

'I'll leave you sandwiches,' Jade had told her.

So here they were, two groups of losers, one from Perth and the other from this poxy village. The ones who'd left school with zero and hadn't found jobs.

Her mum had nodded at the shaved side of Jade's head,

the colour on the other. 'I suppose there's not much you can do about that now. But should you get rid of some of the metalwork, hen?' Indicating the nose- and ear-rings. 'As you've been headhunted.'

'Rounded up, more like.'

The idea was to locate fruit trees in the whole of Perthshire, on public and on private land, in people's gardens. They'd found out which fruit was never collected or eaten or made into anything or even fed to pigs. It was a wasted 'food resource', so they'd been told. Full of Vitamin C and other minerals she'd listed in her jotter. In one village, a walled garden had been discovered with a forgotten orchard inside. And there was 'knowledge and skills' to be woken up about old, funny-named species, how to store and cook the fruit. Recipes for preserves. Yawn, yawn.

'Great for the old CV,' so their supervisor, Rob, had said. 'Speaking to strangers, co-operating with peers. That's "Social Skills".'

'Not slave labour then?' she'd said.

But at the end of each week a payment arrived in her account and it would go on for six months. They'd even had their pictures in the *Perthshire Advertiser*.

She ground the roll-up under the sole of the tiger-patterned DMs she'd finally been able to buy.

'How can you stay here, man?' She said to the lanky guy from the village she'd been paired up with for the day. 'All this fucking green.'

He shrugged at her question, chin dropping into his oversized jacket.

'What's your name again?' she asked.

'Bean.'

She stared at him. Then it clicked; a nickname from school because of his coffee-coloured skin.

'What's to do here?' she pressed.

He looked over his shoulder, shrugged again.

One tearoom, one hotel, probably a church. Was there even a shop? The last shreds of tobacco had gone into her roll-up, so she'd need to scrounge from Bean if there wasn't one.

'Ready?' Rob was herding the pairs towards the gardens they were to survey. Find the fruit trees. Have a chat with the owner. Locate. Pick. 'You're in luck, Bean, teaming up with Jade. Get her to show you her drawings.'

'Fuck off,' she said to Rob's back as he walked away; quietly, mind. Then she shouted: 'What time will we get home?' and texted her mum the answer.

Jade and Bean slouched their way down the short street.

'Jesus, I'm tired,' Jade said. 'Duck in somewhere for a smoke, eh?'

But there was nowhere to go, not even a bench. And Bean just kept walking.

In the garden of the last house, a gnarly old tree stood near the road, thrusting out its branches wide and low and high. Off them dangled great curtains of green, and the trunk, where it was visible, was shaggy with loose, greyish growth.

'This is it,' Bean said. 'Mrs Campbell's.'

'Shitey old mess,' said Jade.

'Just old.'

Bean opened the gate. The grass inside leapt up around their ankles, only lying flat under the tree where it was pressed down by a pool of fallen apples, shining red and green like something out of Snow White. A few fruits still hung in the branches. Bean put his hand out and turned one slightly, unlocking it into his palm, then began picking others into a tote bag.

'You do what you're told, eh? In the country. Well, on you go.' She felt warm sun now on her arms, and pressing on her head. September. Still summer, except with the smell of rotting. 'Wake me up when you're done.'

She lay down in the grass and closed her eyes to a blood-red screen. Began falling backwards into a stuffy sleep.

But then, something rattled on her foot. She opened her eyes to a flare of light and an old woman leaning over her on the path, jabbing her foot with a walking stick. She was squint just like the tree itself, white face folded by age. But she wore a black roll-neck dress that went down to her knees. A red beret, and a dash of red lippie. Jade sat up, sick-feeling and confused. 'What the…?'

'They phoned and told me you were coming. To sort out this poor old thing.' She waved her stick at the tree now. 'It's had to stand in the shadow of the wool mill all those years.'

And then her stick was pointing across the road. Jade turned to follow it, but saw no mill, just an empty space surrounded by a high security fence and hanging from it, a white and red developers' sign which was slipping towards the ground.

'She on something?' she muttered to Bean. 'What fucking mill?'

'Knocked down,' he said quietly. 'When I was wee.'

'"KEEP OUT".' The old woman's mouth wrinkled as she read the sign and snorted quietly to herself, then leant towards Jade and whispered: 'You get youngsters up to no good in the long grass otherwise, eh? Stone's all been taken away to build something else. It's a wasteland waiting for development. Housing probably.'

'Housing?' Jade puzzled at this village stuck in the last century.

'What retards are gonna live there?'

The woman shifted her pale eyes onto Jade, all the wrinkles around her mouth crisping into dark pencil scratches. She had black, arching eyebrows despite the white hair.

'You ask a lot of questions.' She jabbed again at the soles of Jade's boots. 'Get up, get up!'

Jade hauled herself up, as much to get away from her as anything.

The woman prodded her stick towards the tree again now. It was like she was the fucking queen.

'It's had a lifetime not getting any sunlight. And now it's blocking the light from me and my cottage. Getting its own back.' Then she glared at Jade. 'Would the best thing be to chop it down, eh? Give me my view back. It's on its last legs, isn't it?'

'Just needs pruning,' Bean muttered. 'To let the light in.'

The old woman turned her attention to him now.

He looked at his feet.

'What do you know? It's probably ten times your age.'

Jade was able to check out the old woman properly now: the papery skin, a fan of lines branching across each cheekbone. It was kind of disgusting but gripping, like watching a zombie movie. She was obviously ancient, but nothing like Jade's own Nan. And she noticed the woman's hands too, one clasped over the top of the stick; long, knobbly fingers. Hands that looked like they did work.

Bean took out his notepad and showed the old woman a diagram of a tree whose branches were open at the top and then tapered down in a goblet shape to the single trunk. 'Needs done during the winter. Over several winters. Lets the light in and good for wildlife.'

He was a right bloody try-hard.

'I'll come back, if you want. In the winter.'

'You a ventriloquist?' the Campbell woman said to him.

'Sorry?'

'Speaking for what's his name on GQT? The one all the wifies fancy? Greengrass, is it? Bottomflower? You know the one.' The old woman squinted at him. 'I've never seen you at the bridge with the other lads. The ones who drink and chuck cans about the place and all that hooha.'

Jade hovered behind her, miming shoving fingers down her throat, trying to get a reaction from Bean.

'But I did see you once with binoculars beside the loch. Odd thing, that, for a lad, isn't it? At your age.'

Jade prodded at her phone screen, took the call from her mum. She ran through in her head how she'd left things: the walking frame next to the sofa so her mum could tip straight onto it. Nothing blocking the corridor to the bathroom, in case her eyes were funny today, or her balance. A large glass of water and today's meds on the wee table next to her. She'd be waiting for Jade to get back home with the shopping, curtains pulled across even though there was daylight.

'Aye, I'll pick up a kebab on the way. Love you.'

As she had the phone out anyway, Jade opened the app Rob had told them to plot their trees on: 'What3Words'. It identified the location of each three-meter square in the whole world.

'Your tree is at receive.germinate.crumbles,' she told the old woman.

Chill eyes fixed on her, unblinking.

'It's a geolocation app.'

The witchy face puckered into laughter. 'App. Apple. Sap.'

Jade looked away.

She plotted the three words on the data sheet and paused

a moment to see if they stirred any ideas. As part of their 'training', a poet came and did a session with them. They'd gone out into the college grounds and were each told to choose a tree and find the three words for its location. Back inside, they were supposed to write something, poems or wee stories about the place or tree or something they just made up, anything, as long as it included the three words. She'd groaned: 'What's the point? It's like school again.' And put her head down over her arms, doodling into her jotter as she always did; creating a spread of geometric pattern – stars, boxes, triangles, lines in red and green and blue felt pen. She fitted them tightly against each other, stacked them one inside another – triangle within a square, circle with a star in it – covering the double page. She got lost in it.

But when she eventually agreed to write each word down, it was weird because other words came running out of her, not making any sense except at that strike of the moment. And she'd looked up when her attention was called back, and wondered where she was. She'd always enjoyed drawing, but remembered then that at primary school she'd written poems. Hadn't she?

In her jotter she'd made a list of old Scottish apple-names. Her favourite was Bloody Ploughman, which they were told was a tree grown out of the bones of a ploughman caught 'scrumping' apples at some Perthshire castle. What retard would want to eat that one? Then there was Golden Monday, Cambusnethan Pippin, Coul Blush, Lemon Queen, Tower of Glamis, Lady of the Lake.

She'd drawn the shape of each fruit alongside the name and coloured them in. Who knew an apple wasn't just an apple? And not just green. Maybe she could make a rap out of the names.

Mrs Campbell was looming at her again. 'Right odd sort of

youngsters, aren't you, making jam and pruning trees.'

'It's, like, money?' Jade said.

'Used to be you were expected to join up if you couldn't find a job. Males anyway.' She scrutinised Bean, then hunched over her stick, closer to Jade, speaking in a hoarse whisper: 'I was young in the 60s. Ran off to art college in London. I suppose you know what that means?'

Jade stepped back, put her clipboard away into her bag. 'We done, Bean?'

'Skirts up to here.' The old woman cackled and tugged with her stickless hand, hooking her dress above her knees to reveal wrinkled red tights above her boot-tops. 'Of course, the car came before the skirts you know. The "mini".'

Jade looked away.

The woman peered at the apple in Bean's hand. 'So what is it then?'

'A James Grieve,' he said quietly.

She cooed. 'Sounds nice, doesn't he? You can see him in his tweed waistcoat. A polite hat. Probably a gentleman.'

Bean attempted to smile.

'So you'll let some more light into this garden for me? Now you've got the fruit.'

Bean started on about the pruning again, the wildlife, making it clear he wasn't for cutting the tree down. Mr-Ridiculously-Reasonable. It was the most he'd said since Jade met him. She would have been convinced by him, but the old bag wasn't buying it.

'Wildlife? I've already got plenty birds coming to shit in my garden.'

Jade wasn't used to wasting time. Once she'd tried to leave Rob's college-based session early, and he followed her out, asked what her problem was, an edge to his voice. And so she'd told him – straight. Reeled off the list of jobs she had to do at home. He apologised and told her of a service she could call on, to get help for her mum during the day.

'You're alright,' she'd said, looking away up the corridor towards the door out.

'She's entitled to it. And so are you.'

'What notice are they going to take of me?' she said, then told him she'd better go, and felt him watching her stride away, with his hands on his hips.

Jade and Bean prised open one of the security fences opposite the Campbell tree and wriggled through. Plunging away from the road, they hopped between rocks submerged under grass and moss, following a faint path. Tangles of unknown things stuck or hooked themselves to her clothing.

'Shite,' she said when a bramble grabbed her leg. 'I'm bleeding.'

'Stop.' Bean showed her how, if she stopped fighting it, the hooks let her go.

They stood still when they could see the river running brown and frothy.

'Got a fag, Bean?'

He shook his head.

'You what?' she flashed at him.

'Don't smoke.'

Silence slunk around them awhile.

'There a shop?'

He shook his head. 'Not now.'

'Jesus. Fucking. Christ.' She sank down at one end of a large, rectangular block of stone.

He sniggered softly, sat down at the other end. Jade pulled a jotter from her bag, and a pen, started a new page of patterns.

'Where's your house, Bean?'

He pointed vaguely towards a bridge. 'Other side.'

'You come from "the other side", eh? Explains a lot,' she said.

He looked at her, his mouth widening, one end lifted as if trying to work out what she meant. He was quite cute, she noticed, when he smiled. His head bowed again as he grinned down at the rock.

'Got an escape plan?' she asked. 'Out of here?'

He shrugged.

'Something holding you, then?' She wondered whether he had a sick mother too, or a father who needed him to stay. 'If not, get the fuck out of this shit, man.'

She looked up as a line of huge, necky birds came flapping over them, regularly spaced like a line of shapes she might draw in her jotter. She honked back at them. Danced her DMs to their tune.

Then on the far side of the river a great black gaggle of birds erupted from a treetop, flapping and squabbling, massing and remassing.

'Shite. What are they?'

'Corvids.'

'Eh?'

'Crows, rooks, jackdaws.'

'Evil-looking bastards.'

'Clever,' he said.

'How do you know all this shit?'

He laughed.

There was a croaking noise behind them and Jade whirled around.

'So this is where you've got to?'

Old crow Campbell was standing behind them, leaning on her stick.

'Christ,' Jade muttered, turning back to the river and hunching over her jotter again. 'Creepy.'

'Told you this is where they all come. Up to no good. Teenagers.'

Bean gave the old woman a small smile, then turned back as well.

Jade heard the swipe of a stick against dry grass. Some tentative steps. Then Mrs Campbell was turning in to face them. She wobbled suddenly on the uneven ground, and Jade sprang up and thrust her hand under the woman's arm, as if this was her mum. She guided the woman to sit at the centre of the stone, next to Bean.

'Thank you, my dear,' she said, a bit surprised.

'No bother.' It was just a reflex. Jade remained standing. Looked at the time on her phone. She had a while till the minibus would leave but she didn't need to wait here. Let these misfits keep each other company. Next to each other on a stone slab.

'Right,' she said, taking a breath in. But just then the Campbell woman reached deep into a cloth bag slung over her shoulder and pulled out a small silver lighter and a squashy blue packet: *Gitanes*. A bright white cigarette, no filter apparently, was then clamped in her freshly lipsticked mouth.

'Just one a day,' the old woman said. 'Never did get rid of the habit. Could just do with *un petit café* to go with it, eh?'

She offered the packet to Bean next to her, who shook his head. Jade hesitated, a dilemma fighting within her, then snatched one when the packet came to her. She could still leave with it. Had an excuse. Just needed a light.

The old woman patted the gap on the slab to her left. When Jade didn't move, she lit her own, inhaled, chest rising, smoke breathing out.

Jade sat down. Took the lighter from the old woman's hand. Swam away from the weirdness of it all with the first inhale, surprisingly strong. She noticed again the old woman's hands. The skin was a bit like the wrinkled stone they sat on, but lined with blue, yellow, red and all the colours in-between, marking out a webbed pattern.

Some wee bird chattered in a bush. The river did what rivers do. The three of them sat in a row.

'I'll end up with the date printed on my arse,' Mrs Campbell said.

Jade tried not to visualise her arse, an expanse of old, saggy skin. She was ready to leave as soon as the cigarette was finished.

'1831.' Mrs Campbell lifted the cheek next to Jade and pointed at the slab.

She glanced down briefly, saw a 3 and a 1 carved onto the surface. 'That when you were born?'

'Fool.' The woman drew out the o's. 'That's when the mill was built. This old stone was up above the door for over a hundred and eighty years. Imagine that.'

'Fascinating.' Jade caught Bean's eye, and his face lit up again with its crooked grin and then he ducked.

'Much more light since the place came down. It's such a shame nothing's going on here. As if it's cursed ground.' The old woman looked at Jade. 'What would you do with it, my dear, if it was yours?'

'Build a shop that sells tobacco.'

Mrs Campbell laughed.

'Or a pub. A nightclub.'

'They've got that down by the bridge haven't they, young man? Mallarkying about with the mallards.'

Jade stood up now, ground the cigarette butt under a DM. 'I'll see you then. Thanks for the apples.' She picked up the tote bag. 'And the fag.'

'There's a secret on the other side, I believe.' Mrs Campbell leaned forward as if it shouldn't be heard.

'Other side of what?'

She pointed one, yellow-grained finger at the rock beneath her. 'Want to see?'

'I'll leave that treat for Bean.' Jade laughed. 'I'm away.'

'There's another fag in it for you. And anyway, it needs both of you to turn it,' Mrs Campbell said and held out a hand, apparently expecting a pull up, a gesture familiar to Jade from her mother. So her hand went out again without thinking. Then Bean was up too.

Mrs Campbell stood like a conductor, prodding her stick first at the rock, then tap-tapping on Bean's arm. 'A bit of muscle, is there?'

Jade made sure she stood just out of reach.

'Just roll it over,' the old woman said, pointing at the stone.

Both stared at her.

'Why?' Jade asked.

'Come on, get your young backs into it.'

'Sake,' Jade muttered.

But they knelt down and scrabbled fingers into damp, sluggy grass, trying to get purchase. Bean found a plank of wood and wedged it under as a lever, and up it rose like a lid.

Jade felt a tremor at what they were going to find there; treasure or a passageway or even a grave. And then the balance seemed to shift in the stone so that it took on its own life and rolled over by itself, leaving the underneath side facing upwards and a dark earthy rectangle where it had been, straggled with white roots. A crowd of confused slaters scuttled away, seeking the dark again.

'Jeez!'

'Brush it off. So we can see.'

Bean used his sleeve to scatter clods of soil, and revealed the new surface, smoother than the side they'd used as a seat.

'Now your turn, young woman.'

'Jade's the name.'

'Well, Jade, it's called "frottage". You know it? Basic printmaking. You've got paper, haven't you? Soft pencil? B, 2B. 4B?'

Jade looked at her blankly until the old woman pulled a pencil from her own bag. 'Paper!' she ordered. 'Put it over the marks there and then rub the lead over it.'

'I've got to get the minibus.'

'One minute it will take. Remember there's a fag in it for you.'

Jade looked at the exposed face of stone. It would be good to have another smoke before the journey home. So she rubbed at the tendrils of greyish green which came off easily, and now saw a faint, carved line; rubbed her sleeve across it, found two more. The three lines together formed a narrow triangle. There was more, but it was difficult to make out. Straight lines branching off each other like a tree.

'Shit,' she said. 'Weird.'

She tore a page from her jotter and laid it over the carving, then with the soft pencil rubbed furiously over the whole area.

More appeared on paper than had been visible on the stone itself. A smaller triangle met the large one, tip to tip, and there were lines striking away from both.

She held up the black scratched page, and then turned it so

that at the top was the small triangle. Three chips had been carved inside it. Hardly anything. And yet it was somehow obvious what it represented:

eye   eye
mouth

'It's a face,' Jade shrieked. 'It's a fucking face.'

The rest of the figure now materialised around the face. A long, slim triangle for a dress, legs and arms made with simple chipped lines, and another set of lines radiating from the top of the triangular face: hair. She held up the page in triumph as if she'd made the image herself. A figure in negative, and weirdly alive. You could tell it belonged to someone you wouldn't mess with.

'Look at that!' The old woman crowed. 'You'll be going to art college next, young lady.'

She leant close to Jade who looked into the old woman's face, finding herself transfixed by the deep lines carved onto it, just like the stone itself. She could smell stale tea on her breath.

The woman fixed her with pale crow eyes. 'Go on. Run away to London like I did,' she hissed.

'London?' Jade just managed to hold back the 'fuck off' that wanted to spit itself out.

'Well at least Edinburgh.'

There was no point explaining. There never was. Or, nearly never. Jade imagined her mother's terrified face if she said she was leaving. She'd try to be brave, tell Jade to get on with her life, sacrifice herself probably. But there would never be enough money to provide twenty-four-hour care. And where would college fees come from?

The three of them sat in a row again.

'Who's she?' Bean asked. 'The figure?'

Mrs Campbell shrugged. 'The green maiden, I suppose. A *glaistig*.'

'What's that?' Jade asked.

'A sort of green witch.'

Jade felt a surprising shudder pass through her. 'What's she doing on a stone?'

'That's going to have to be one of those mysteries,' Mrs Campbell said. 'I hear you're turning my apples into preserves. Why don't you put her on your jam jars?'

'Who wants a witch hanging out on their jam?' Jade said.

Mrs Campbell peered at her. 'A witch is just another word for a strong woman. A determined one. People have always been scared of them. They're probably scared of you.'

'I'm no witch.'

'Well look what you've magicked up.'

When she pointed, Jade held up the page of her jotter again for them to admire.

'Going to enter the competition?' Bean asked.

Jade settled her gaze on him. His quizzical eyes. That smile. 'Fuck off.' She closed her jotter.

Bean explained to Mrs Campbell that there had been a Perthshire-wide call for apple-squad members to come up with a 'brand' for the fruit products. An image for the logo, and a name that would go on all the labels on jars and bottles.

'Something historical, perhaps?' Rob had suggested to Jade's group. 'Something to do with trees or gardens?'

It had to have a catchy name, they kept being told. The session got yawningly boring.

'No imagination between the lot of you,' Rob had said. And they made it a competition instead with various opportunities and even some cash as a prize.

'I reckon she'd be just the ticket. Green Witch Jams and Pickles,' Mrs Campbell said. 'You could make a better print. Use green ink, my dear.'

'How do we do that?' Jade asked.

'Graphics app,' Bean said.

'You got one?' Jade asked.

Bean nodded. 'Take five minutes.'

Jade looked at her watch, suddenly thinking of her mum, waiting for her, perhaps sitting in the dark with the TV on. 'I'm a thorn in your side, love,' she'd said that morning. Had she left the glass of water close enough for her mum to reach?

'So how come you're here, anyway? If you ran away to London?' Jade said.

Mrs Campbell was obviously a failure. Back here. *Tail between her legs,* as her mum would say.

'Why wouldn't I be here?'

'It's fucking dead.' Jade flicked a hand around.

The woman raised up her knobbly hands and looked back at the dark crags and the river never pausing in front. When Jade looked at Bean, he was looking up too at a single dark bird. The air was so still you could hear its feathers whispering.

Jade felt like the two of them were doing something religious. She stood up.

'You mean, you actually wanted to be here?' she challenged. 'Rather than be an artist?'

Mrs Campbell laughed. 'Exhibited all over the world, my dear.'

'You?' It leapt out before she could catch it. 'Here?'

'This place was my source.'

'Paintings?'

'Prints mostly. These days, especially.'

Jade stared at Mrs Campbell, whose shape seemed to have altered into something more interesting.

Mrs Campbell took an apple from her bag and handed it to Bean who looked at Jade, miming incomprehension with his screwed-up face.

'Got a knife, son?'

He took out his pruning knife, put the apple on the stone, and was about to slice it from stem to tail.

'Not that way,' the old woman commanded.

Bean hovered the knife over it for a moment as he stared at the apple and then he cut it in half around its equator, and peered at the new pale surfaces. With his one-sided grin beginning to curl, he turned a pale circle towards Jade and the old woman.

'That's it.' The woman took it from his hand.

The three of them peered down at the almost luminous circle of white flesh. At its centre the seed case formed a dark, perfect, five-pointed star.

'Shit. How did you do that?' It felt to Jade like another trick had been performed. A few scratches on stone had become a defiant woman. A backwater; a place for artists. An apple could give you a star within a circle.

The old woman pointed to where two browny-red seeds were edging out of the star-case, as if about to fall to the earth.

'One for each of you two, eh?'

'Two trees?' asked Jade.

'Promise to be, I would guess, if looked after right. Young Flowerdew there can tell you how, I'm sure.'

Jade and Bean leaned in from either side of her, looked up at each other, and then an agreement seemed to bind them in a blink. Jade had already been mentally doodling a label in her jotter. Now she could envisage a living thing growing out of the ground; branching out.

All three of them turned and looked down at the dark rectangle in front of them where the stone had laid before. Bare soil exposed to the light.

And it was obvious where the apple trees should grow.

Acknowledgments

This book began twenty years ago as a novel with the support of a Scottish Arts Council bursary and the blessing of Literature Officer, Gavin Wallace. Some core elements of the novel have survived in much reduced form, and other characters have since woven their way into the story. This means that over the years I've had feedback on the manuscript and support with background research from many people, as well as a residency at Brownsbank Cottage, and a Royal Literary Fund Fellowship during the writing process.

I'd like to thank the Soutar House Writing Group in Perth for feedback at the beginning of the process, both its then members and associated writers-in-residence Carl MacDougall and Brian McCabe. Later, the women's writing group in Glasgow led by Elizabeth Reeder; Perthshire writers Polly Pullar, Jamie Grant and Ruary Mackenzie Dodds, and more recently the Birnam Writers' Group. Also to Sam Boyce, Jenny Brown and Liz Small for editorial advice, and to readers Claire Squires and Robin Dance for encouraging me to believe it could be a book.

Specialised input came from stonemason Martin Reilly, architects Joann Russell and Robin Baker, and Dr Billy Kenefick of Dundee University. Other insights were provided by the Perth & Kinross Council Archives at the AK Bell Library in Perth, and P and J Haggart woollen manufacturers (now

Glenlyon Tweed Mill), Aberfeldy.

I'm particularly grateful to Patrick Jamieson, Dani Silva, Robert Alan Jamieson and Jennie Renton for the creative enterprise of Taproot Press and their enthusiasm for this book.

A number of the stories have been previously published, as follows:

'Stone Curse' (as 'The Other Side of Stone') in *She Said, He Said, I Said, New Writing Scotland 35*, Ed. Diana Hendry, Susie Maguire, ASLS, 2017.

'In and Out the Windows', *Work* anthology, Ed. Bernard MacLaverty, Polygon, 2006.

'The Last Tweed', Scottish Arts Council online showcase, 2008.

'The Lost Son' in *Story*, the online home of the Save the Short Story Campaign, Book Trust, 2008.

About the Author

Linda Cracknell is a writer of fiction, non-fiction and drama for whom landscape, place and memory are key themes. She lives in Highland Perthshire, Scotland, but her writing and teaching take her to different landscapes, including to the sea and the Sahara.

www.lindacracknell.com

Previous Publications

Life Drawing, Neil Wilson Publishing, 2000.
Short Story collection.

The Searching Glance, Salt Publishing, 2008.
Short story collection.

A Wilder Vein, Two Ravens Press, 2009.
Editor, anthology of non-fiction writing about the wild places of the British Isles.

Call of the Undertow, Freight, 2013.
Novel.

Doubling Back: Ten Paths Trodden in Memory, Freight, 2014.
Narrative non-fiction.

The publication of *The Other Side of Stone* and other Taproot Press 2021 titles owes special thanks to the following book bundle subscribers:

Duncan McLean, Orkney
James Robertson, Newtyle
Jonathan Swale, Shetland
Wilma Jamieson, Edinburgh
Flo Cairns, Scotland
Hanne Tange, Aarhus, Denmark
Grace and Iain Macniven, Scotland
Elena Soper, Linlithgow
C. McKinnell, Edinburgh
Hazel B. Anderson, Bressay, Shetland
Christine Hunter, Newquay

Upcoming 2021 Titles from Taproot Press

Open Secret: Hong Kong Since the Umbrella Movement edited by Tammy Lai-Ming Ho and Dexter Yim

Hard Roads an Cauld Hairst Winds: Li Bai an Du Fu in Scots owreset bi Brian Holton